"I love this book. Fun to read about the truth and zaniness of living on a faraway island in the huge Pacific. Race is smart, insightful and totally interesting."
— CASSIE HAMMAN, FREELANCE, NEWSPAPERS AND MAGAZINES

"Another group of fun stories about the islands with Tom Parker and Carlos Montano. It's just the book you need when sitting at the beach bar and sipping an ice cold beer. Very entertaining."
— JOHN BOWE, AUTHOR OF *GIG* AND *No Bodies*

"When you don't have time or money for travel, read Race's novel and you can feel the sun on your face, and the sand between your toes It's fun and light Of course, the bad guys get it in the end."
— FRED PRICE, AUTHOR OF *Lair of the Dragon* AND *Dragon's Ghost*

"The book is authentic. Race has lived in the islands with the local people. You will enjoy it for sure."
— BOB COLDEEN, AUTHOR OF *Saipan Baseball* AND *Bumps in the Road*

"I really enjoyed reading about the stories in the islands. There are dozens more to record. I'll tell Race some ancient legends when we next share a beer."
— BENSEN, 80-YEAR-OLD STORYTELLER AT AMERICAN MEMORIAL PARK

"It's good to see the hoodlums taken out. I enjoyed the whole book, especially the local island humor and taking a trip to the Philippines."
— PAUL G. PETREDIS, AUTHOR OF *Escape from North Korea*

"Joe Race knows police work and the islands. The combination makes for good reading and interesting, realistic characters. A good read."
— BRYAN VILA, AUTHOR OF *Tired Cops* AND *Capital Punishment in the United States*

OTHER TITLES BY JOE RACE

MOVIN' ON

MOON OVER MANILA (January 2008)

CONTINUIN' ON

ENJOYING BURSTS OF HAPPINESS
AND FINDING TRUE ADVENTURE

Order this book online at www.trafford.com/07-1807
or email orders@trafford.com

Most Trafford titles are also available at major online book retailers.

© Copyright 2007 Joe Race.

All rights reserved. No part of this publication may be reproduced, stored in a retrieval system, or transmitted, in any form or by any means, electronic, mechanical, photocopying, recording, or otherwise, without the written prior permission of the author.

Author's photograph by Griz Miradora, Saipan – <Gresil317@hotmail.com>

Front cover painting "Washed Ashore" by Joe Weaver, Saipan artist – <www.joeweaver.net>

Note for Librarians: A cataloguing record for this book is available from Library and Archives Canada at www.collectionscanada.ca/amicus/index-e.html

Printed in Victoria, BC, Canada.

ISBN: 978-1-4251-4320-6

We at Trafford believe that it is the responsibility of us all, as both individuals and corporations, to make choices that are environmentally and socially sound. You, in turn, are supporting this responsible conduct each time you purchase a Trafford book, or make use of our publishing services. To find out how you are helping, please visit www.trafford.com/responsiblepublishing.html

Our mission is to efficiently provide the world's finest, most comprehensive book publishing service, enabling every author to experience success. To find out how to publish your book, your way, and have it available worldwide, visit us online at www.trafford.com/10510

 www.trafford.com

North America & international
toll-free: 1 888 232 4444 (USA & Canada)
phone: 250 383 6864 ♦ fax: 250 383 6804 ♦ email: info@trafford.com

The United Kingdom & Europe
phone: +44 (0)1865 722 113 ♦ local rate: 0845 230 9601
facsimile: +44 (0)1865 722 868 ♦ email: info.uk@trafford.com

10 9 8 7 6 5 4 3 2 1

DEDICATION

Beaucoup thanx to my wife Salve'

*... the patience of a saint,
the beauty of an Egyptian queen,
and the drive of a* CEO...

POTPOURRI

EDUCATION   *"Only the educated are free."*
                 —EPICTETUS, FIRST CENTURY

DANGER   *"The world is a dangerous place to live—not because of the people who are evil, but because of the people who don't do anything abut it."*
                 —ALBERT EINSTEIN

HONESTY   *"I never give them hell. I just tell the truth, and they think it is hell."*
                 —PRESIDENT HARRY S. TRUMAN

INTEGRITY   *"To keep your character intact, you cannot stoop to filthy acts. It °makes it easier to stoop the next time..."*
                 —KATHARINE HEPBURN

SERVICE   *"Service is not a chore, service is a privilege."*
                 —MOTHER THERESA

SUCCESS   *The average man who wins what we call success is not a genius. He is a man who has merely the ordinary qualities that he shares with his fellows, and who has developed those ordinary qualities to a more than ordinary degree."*
                 —PRESIDENT THEODORE ROOSEVELT

UNDERSTATEMENT "*Nothing of importance happened today.*"
—A NOTE IN THE DIARY OF KING GEORGE II OF ENGLAND ON JULY 4, 1776

WORLD'S FIRST
KNOWN NOVEL *Cyropaedia by the Greek writer Xenophon, about 360 B.C. It is about the life of Cyrus, founder of the Persian Empire. It considers a positive view of Persian society, contrasting with the negative views by most Greeks. Great lessons in government, military science and political philosophy. Read extensively by Caesar and Machiavelli.*

WORRIES "I am an old man and have known a great many troubles, but most of them have never happened."
—MARK TWAIN

TABLE OF CONTENTS

	DEDICATION	5
	POTPOURRI	6
	PROLOGUE	11
1	WATCHING THE BEACH	14
2	THE BATTERED AMATEUR PROSTIE	18
3	THE GROUND COLLAPSES	24
4	THE MAVEN PAYS A VISIT	30
5	GOT BETEL NUT?	37
6	THE ISLAND WET T-SHIRT CONTEST	43
7	FALSE SELLING TO YAKUZA	53
8	SAILING WITH THE AUSSIES	59
9	SWEPT OFF THE ROCKS	66
10	LEO GOES SWIMMING	74
11	OFF TO THE PHILIPPINES	81

12	THE PROLIFIC MAYOR	86
13	DINA IS MISSING ON SAIPAN	91
14	FINDING DINA	95
15	WHITEY ESCAPES FROM THE ZOO	101
16	SKULL TO THE CRIME LAB	107
17	DIGGING UP THE BODIES	115
18	BUTCH SOLVES ID THEFT CASE	119
19	MWARS-MWARS AND PONYTAILS	124
20	NEW BBQ STAND	134
21	MANGKUKULAM VISITS MARY	138
22	THE SUNKEN NUESTA SENORA DE LA CONCEPTION	142
23	THE POSSE DECIDES TO PARTY	149
24	THE SUN-TANNED GIRLS	154
25	IDENTIFICATION AND TRIAL	162
26	JILL FINDS LOVE AND COMMITMENT	167
27	FIVE DOWN – THREE TO GO	174
28	THE USELESS FAT PROSECUTOR	181
29	TANO ANTIGO v. MABUHAY POWER	191
30	THE THREE BROS	198
31	MAMA-SAN AND THE GIRLS	208
32	FUNNY MONEY – STRANGE LITTLE MAN	213
33	THE COMMISH	218
34	THE LAST ASSHOLE	223
	EPILOGUE	228
	GLOSSARY	232
	ACKNOWLEDGMENTS	238

PROLOGUE

Although this is a work of fiction, Saipan does in fact exist as the capital of the Commonwealth of the Mariana Islands, a group of fourteen islands north of Guam. The local people are US citizens but the majority of 70,000 residents in the CNMI are guest workers from other countries, such as the Philippines, China, Japan , Sri Lanka, Bangladeshi, Nepal, Russia and other geographical areas on the globe. They were brought here for farming, hotel workers, and garment manufacturing. Some stayed over as tourists. This unusual population analysis is similar to Kuwait's, in that the outside worker population is larger than that of the indigenous peoples.

You'll recognize the characters from my first book, *Movin' On*, such as narrator Tom Parker who retired as a Sheriff's Sergeant from "the mean, ugly streets of Los Angeles and traveled to the warm, sandy beaches of Micronesia." He won a huge jackpot in Las Vegas and wandered off to the tropics in search of paradise, and ended up buying a rundown 88-room hotel,

The Beach Hotel, on Saipan during bad economic times.

You'll know the efficient Hotel Manager Cocina Parker right away, his new Filipina wife and her three children Annie, Donna and Anthony, who Tom adopts and treasures as his own. You'll remember Chamorro warrior Carlos Montano, Tom's good friend and partner in the International Private Investigations Agency, based at the hotel.

The hotel has its regular cast of characters, Myla, Lola, Masako, Aubrey, Yoshi, Mario I, and Mario II. You'll enjoy reading about the head chef Guangman, and his athletic wife, Seuchill and their daughter Bora. George and Jo, and their matchmaker and marriage business are back on deck, as are Lawyer Ernie Martines, and his wife Anita. Kaylene is still managing her successful tailoring shop.

The Beachologist, Fred Cannon and his wife Mae and his musical group are back with us. Mama-san Chang and two of her girls, Wang Ren and Little Ling are still renting two hidden back rooms for their special Japanese visitors. The computer wizard of the islands, Butch, helps Tom and Carlos solve a case. The ship-wrecked Jill Flannigan discovers love again and finds herself leaving her transition man, tennis pro Jonah.

Expect to find another array of interesting characters from as far away as the Philippines and Australia. Running a hotel and an investigations agency, and raising children, and entertaining Tom's two brothers, will offer an opportunity to introduce new and exciting characters, some outright evil. Take a look at the glossary at the back of the novel for a quick translation of some of the words used in Saipan's multi-cultural environment.

Enjoy and remember, the hammock is reserved with your name. We have our share of mosquitoes, cockroaches, rats, power

Continuin' On

outages, typhoons, and coconuts falling on your head. But when you're sitting on the LA freeway, or caught up in a New York snow storm, think of deep-blue skies, pink sunsets, wide-open spaces, and warm, balmy breezes. The average annual temperature is 84 degrees, night and day — the same temp in the lagoon ocean water. There's probably a vacant room at the inn — just call Cocina.

Serendipity awaits.

I

WATCHING THE BEACH

I was sitting on the balcony of my hotel penthouse, smoking a Filipino deluxe cigar, and watching the sea birds dipping and diving in the ocean for a mid-day meal. It was another one of those typical gorgeous days in paradise. The big, white fluffy clouds were billowing and bouncing off the horizon. I was supervising the beach. I am very dedicated to my job. Saipan is a wonderful place to live and relax.

Our three children were off at school. I was taking an afternoon siesta after helping my wife, Cocina, finish up the month-end bills for our hotel. She was satisfied with the 90% occupancy rate, and knew that we were beginning to turn a healthy profit for all our hard work the previous year. Just as we predicted, eco-tourism was popular and attracting guests from all the world. Tourists wanted a little adventure with their trips, and were equally concerned about the future of the oceans and the fragile reefs.

Cocina was relieved that our son, Anthony, had fully recovered

Continuin' On

after being shot by an assailant, whom I had been investigating for drug sales, bribery and fraud. My money manager in Los Angeles, financial wizard Angel Cho, said that I was right on track in doubling my millions. Our in-house accountant Mario I was doing a bang-up job and worked closely with Angel on a monthly basis. I was trying not to be one of those worry-warts that get all nervous and jumpy when things are just going too well.

This was a long way from the mean, dangerous streets of South Los Angeles. I had survived physically and emotionally after twenty years of fighting gangs and trying to suppress the high homicide rate. The big win in Las Vegas at the slots gave me this new start in life… and maybe karma.

The hotel was in tiptop shape after the maintenance and security supervisor, Mario II, selected the right people for the jobs, and trained them, and got the supplies that they needed. The bright rose-colored paint job on the hotel reminded our guests of the Navajo pueblos in New Mexico. Thanks to Yoshi, the new landscaping was immaculate, and much appreciated by the tourists, especially the senior citizens coming regularly from Japan. In December, they came from the cold, snowy mountains of Sapporo into our warm Garden of Eden, with its thousands of colorful flowers. Their cameras get a real workout.

I watched Lola cleaning and manicuring the beach to perfection. The white lounging chairs were laid out in perfect symmetry. The hammocks were freshly washed. She took a personal interest in how the beach looked, and worked steadily without any supervision. Our Korean chef, Guangman, was the same way in the kitchen. He was continually creating and serving the most luscious, scrumptious dishes. When Carlos and I hit it big on the fishing boat, we'd take our catch to the hotel kitchen.

His favorite question always was, "Boss how do you want the fish prepared? You want it barbequed, baked, sautéed, fricasseed, deep-fried, sashimi and sushi style, stewed, or grilled?" My response was usually to the effect, "Use your own judgment. How do you remember all that?" Guangman's wife Seuchill and their child Bora were two of the top female athletes on Saipan. Mostly they were the jocks of the family, while Guangman liked to do needlepoint and *origami*. They helped out in the kitchen when Guangman and his assistant Miguel, were overwhelmed with a full hotel or a celebration.

Most all of our employees were working at a high level of competence. I knew that the profit-sharing, bonus plan helped to motivate the work ethic, but I also knew that Cocina was a fair and likeable boss. As I had planned from the beginning, "The Beach Hotel" partially belonged to the employees, and they believed in the motto for our guests "Your Home for Fun and Health." They had a vested interest.

I left the penthouse, and used the six levels of stairs going down for exercise. I walked past the pool. There were dozens of guests playing and tanning, and the pool was crystal clear, and the sharpest *azul* blue of the spectrum. I waved at Cocina in her office in the lobby area, as I walked into my PI office next door, the International Private Investigations Agency. My friend and fellow detective, Carlos Montano, was on the phone having an intense conversation. He had just returned from a temporary job working as a Deputy Chief for six months at the Department of Public Safety. He had previously retired from the Attorney General's Office as a Senior Investigator, but had gone back to help out the new commissioner at DPS, until she got her new command staff hired and trained.

Continuin' On

I whispered to Carlos, "What have you got? Need a diversion to get you off the phone?"

He nodded, and mouthed, "Its okay, Tom. We're almost done."

As he was hanging up the phone, he said, "Yeah…right… I'll tell Tom Parker that you called. Yeah…yeah…" to the other person on the phone. He shook his head.

I asked, "What was that all about?"

Carlos replied, "Just an asshole lawyer. You know Jim Walcott. He's representing one of the crooked DPS cops, and he wants us to reconsider several of the charges. He knows better than to call me. I told him to get hold of the prosecutor. He said that he already tried that, but it was a no-go."

I said, "You did right, amigo. He knows he has to go to the prosecutor to adjust court charges."

Carlos added, "Wolcott said his client, Sonny Ramirez, is going to be real mad. I asked Wolcott if I should take that as a threat or just a thought in passing." Carlos had picked up his ever-present baseball bat, and was taking practice swings.

I smiled, "And how did he answer that?"

"That's about when you walked in, Tom. He stammered and stuttered a little, and said that he didn't mean anything. He was just thinking about his client."

I said, "Outa our hands. Fuck him and the horse he rode in on. Let the lawyers work it out. Meanwhile, what do we have on the agenda today in the PI business?"

I noticed that Carlos' desk was covered with pages of notes from ubiquitous yellow pads. Several of them had doodling and scribbling, and a few had legible phone numbers.

2

THE BATTERED AMATEUR PROSTIE

I asked, looking at the pads, "Carlos, what's all that? Is it the next case?"

"Negative, Tom. Not to worry. Its notes from my computer class. I'm still trying to get proficient with that crazy mystery box. We can't rely on Cocina and your daughter, Annie, all the time."

"Good on ya. I know that I've got to get past simple word processing, especially when we have to analyze some of our fraud cases. But maybe I'll just stay ignorant and let you do all the work. You be a college graduate."

Carlos laughed, sorting out his notes, "You probably don't want to rely on me for real important cases."

The phone rang.

I said, "The public calls. I'll get it."

Carlos said, "If it's Walcott, tell him that I've gone home to sort out my sock drawer."

It wasn't Walcott. It was a very upset Chinese man named Tse Chin. He said that his cousin, Mai Lee, had been raped

CONTINUIN' ON

and assaulted, and the police wouldn't do anything about it. I told him to come down to the PI office, and that we would talk to him. I also cautioned him that it sounded like a police matter, and maybe he should talk to a supervisor at the police station.

Tse and Mai were at the office in fifteen minutes. Tse was a tall, handsome man, and Mai was likely very beautiful. But she had been severely beaten. Her face was swollen and misshapen, and an eye closed. She had deep bruise marks on her neck. Carlos took a series of photos with his digital camera.

We did the introductions, and Carlos got everyone a cold coconut drink. Mai spoke very little English. Tse started off by saying that Mai had lost her job to cutbacks in the garment factory, and that she had gone out on a date with a local Chamorro man, Juan Riviera. She knew the man from the factory, and he said that he would help her buy food and some medicine for her baby boy. She went along with the man, and he stopped his truck on a beach far from any houses. He then gave her twenty dollars, and had sex with her. That part of it was consensual.

Tse then said, "Mai didn't resist the man because she needed the money for food and medicine, and the rent was due. To be honest, she'd done this before with several men. She had her regulars. She always needed to send money home because her father was ill."

He continued, "But she was naïve about her own safety. This time the man called his friends on his phone, and soon the truck was surrounded with six other local men. Juan pulled her out of his truck, and pushed her down on the sand. He then told all his friends that they could fuck her, because he had already paid. The men tore off all her clothing."

Tse said that Mai tried to run away, but they grabbed her and threw her back down. They were on a remote beach, and no one could hear her screams. Several of the men punched her, and told her to stop resisting. Mai was bleeding from her mouth, and three teeth were knocked loose. She was terrified and in a dazed mental state. She didn't remember everything, except apparently all the men took turns having sex with her. Several of the men had ejaculated on her face and hair.

Tse said that after the sex, the men talked about just leaving her or killing her, and throwing her in the ocean. She understood little about what they were saying, but she knew that they were talking about her, because they kept looking at her. They were all excited, and wildly gesturing, and she heard the word "witness." She was still lying on the sand, naked. One of the men came over, and fucked her again. Another man came over, and slapped her, almost into near unconsciousness. He called her, 'his little bitch." She managed to gather up her clothing, and ran through the jungle to Tse's house.

Tse added, "I think they let her go, because she was so afraid, and wouldn't call the police. They also knew that she spoke limited English, and that even with a translator, the police wouldn't believe her, or care, because she took money for sex. Some of the police consider prosties to be useless, throw-away people. Besides, she is Chinese, and very low in the pecking order. Right now, she wants to erase the whole thing from her mind."

I said, "That's normal. Most women just want to forget, or even move to another town or leave home. There's the embarrassment, and the worry that they might be impregnated with one of the attacker's baby, or maybe diseased. Some of these assholes would fuck a patient at a VD clinic, and never think of using a condom."

Continuin' On

Mai began to sob, and her body shuddered. When Carlos went to soothe her, she jumped back and her eyes glazed over. She snarled like a mad dog. He backed away, and said, "Sorry, I mean you no harm. I just want to help." Carlos is a huge Chamorro man, and could be scary to anyone.

She looked at him, then Tse and me, and saw that it was okay. She gave Carlos a weak smile.

I asked, "Can she identify the men, or at least Juan, the man from the factory?"

Tse answered, "She's knows Juan and his family, and knows one of the men that raped her. His name is Ricardo, and lives near her apartment. She thinks he was the one trying to save her from being killed."

I asked, "Will she testify? That's going into a court of law and pointing out the assholes?"

Tse spoke to her in Mandarin Chinese, and she nodded that she would.

I asked if she had showered and cleaned up after the rape, and Tse said that she had just wiped herself off. Tse said that he also saved the clothing that she had been wearing.

I called Commissioner Lois Harding at the police station, and explained the situation. Lois said that she would send over two of her trustworthy investigators and get the job done. I told her that they could have a private hotel room for the interview, and that Carlos' Chinese wife, Daisy, could do the translation. Mai could stay in the room in seclusion until she was comfortable going out again around the island.

We took Mai to the hospital. Lois assigned a female officer to meet with Tse and Mai. With the help of the ER doctor and an experienced RN, valuable pieces of evidence were obtained and saved from Mai's person, such as fibers, blood, semen, and pubic hairs. She had managed to scratch several of her attackers, and this blood and flesh residue was gathered from her fingernails. Tse gave the torn clothing to the female officer. Several semen and blood stains were evident. DNA would help put the assailants in the jailhouse.

Within seven hours, all six men were identified. As is the case with most accomplices, one suspect led to the next suspect, and they out-ratted each other in blaming everyone except themselves. Lois had the airport and seaport sealed immediately, and theoretically it was impossible to leave the island. Arrest warrants were served, and the suspects were all in custody within two days. Several of the men had scratched faces, just as Mai had said.

Rivera tried to get by on the flimsy excuse that he had only committed a misdemeanor by paying Mai for sex, and that she was equally guilty. He said that he had no responsibility for what happened next when all his friends assaulted and raped her. That didn't fly with the lady judge who had all the suspects jailed with a $50,000 bail on each.

Five weeks passed. As the court arraignment neared, the prosecutor wanted to re-interview Mai and let her know what he would be asking in court. He also wanted Mai to be comfortable with the government translator. Her phone was disconnected and the investigators went out to find her. She was gone, as was her baby son. The investigators checked with the immigration officers, and discovered that she had departed to China two days before. She didn't tell Tse about her plans.

The following day, Mai telephoned Tse, and said that her parents had raised money in China for her ticket home. Her parents had advised her to get home before the trial, or she would

Continuin' On

be arrested for prostitution, or the local men would arrange to have her killed. She was also worried that the authorities would take away her baby boy, and judge her to be an unfit mother. The suspects had impregnated her in the rape, but she had taken some Chinese medicine which aborted the fetus. Her wounds had healed nicely, and her loosened teeth had naturally tightened back up.

Mai asked that Tse pass along her gratitude to Carlos and me, and the Commissioner. Tse said that she was crying and distraught, and she begged that we understand her situation. We understood, but didn't like what would happen next.

Three days later with no witness or victim to testify, seven violent felons walked out of the courtroom, free to roam the beaches again. A different form of animal, but the saber tooth tigers are still waiting in the dark.

3

THE GROUND COLLAPSES

Anthony was growing emotionally and physically. For a 13-year-old, he was mature, and it showed in his good grades, and his ability to get along with everyone. He recovered nicely after being shot by the miscreants and now had full use of his shoulders and arms. Derek Palacios, living five houses south of the hotel, and three years younger, became Anthony's good buddy. We took to calling Derek "the Shadow', because he was forever following Anthony, and even began to mimic Anthony's manner of speaking and walking and making hand gestures.

Towards late afternoon with a break in the wet weather, Anthony and Derek decided to ride their mountain bicycles up over the hills along the coastline. The boys had taken this same ride dozens of times, and they actually fashioned a trail that paralleled the beach and went over the small hills. Tourists and hikers used the trail quite often. Anthony told his sister, Donna, that they'd be gone for two hours, and would be back for dinner.

Continuin' On

The ride did not go well for the boys. It had rained steadily off and on for the past two weeks, and the ground was saturated. It was a tough ride for the boys through the sand and hillside clay. Rather than going over one of the hills, Anthony led out around the hill by going inland about one hundred yards. He was in front of Derek by about twenty yards. Suddenly the earth broke loose under his bicycle, and along with a ton of soil and rock, Anthony tumbled downward into a huge cave. He fell about forty feet into a large pool of water. He was covered with sand and mud, but wasn't hit by any coral or rock. He felt his bicycle land on top of him but the water above him broke the impact. As he surfaced through the water, he knew he was in part of the ocean. The water was salty, and he could feel the water moving back and forth, like the movement of the tide. It felt that he was trapped in a giant washing machine. He looked up and around, and could only see light at the top of the cave.

Derek looked over the edge, and said, "Anthony, are you there? Are you okay?"

"Yeah, I'm fine. I don't feel any bones broken, and I don't have any large cuts."

There were no trees or plants, or driftwood that he could grab hold of to help climb out of the cave. The sides of the cave were polished smooth by the constant water action inside the cave.

Derek crawled close, trying to see Anthony down below. He yelled out that he would go for help. He was on top of some wet clay. As he turned to leave, his feet began to slide, and he wasn't able to stop or grab onto anything to break his fall. He fell headfirst into the cave, landing a few feet from Anthony in the pool of water.

Anthony asked, "Are you okay? That was big splash!"

"Yeah, I'm fine. Just trying to get my air back." The boys had to tread water, as the water was getting deeper as the tide was filling in the cave.

Anthony said, "Now we've got a major problem. Who can go for help? Maybe they won't even miss us until dark, and won't be able to find us until morning. They might not even see your bicycle on top."

Derek's eyes got larger, and his bottom lip began to quiver from fear, and the colder water in the cave. Both boys were physically fit and good swimmers, but the possibility of treading water for many hours was not tenable. They also felt a strong undertow in the cave as the tide was surging, which was threatening to drag them back under the cave walls into remote tunnels and unknown channels directly into the open sea.

Anthony noticed that the tide was raising them higher into the cave, but even with a high tide, he knew that they would still be 25-30 feet from the top of the cave. They tried yelling, but the crashing and banging of the waves and undertow in the cave covered over their voices. There were no finger or toe holds on the side of the cave.

An hour passed, and they heard someone yelling from the top. It was an Asian language, maybe Japanese, and the boys yelled back. During the lull of crushing water against the sides of the cave, Anthony heard a man and woman's voice, and he thought the man said something like, *"Daijo'obu tassuke-te."* It sounded re-assuring.

The man and woman were guests at The Beach Hotel, and wheeled Derek's bicycle quickly back to the hotel where our beach supervisor, Lola, was straightening up everything at beachside at the end of the day. Lola knew very little Japanese, so she used her

Continuin' On

cell phone and called my wife and hotel manager, Cocina, who spoke passable "hotel" Japanese. Cocina was at the beach in a flash, and immediately identified Derek's bicycle. The Japanese couple explained what they had seen and heard, and offered to guide Cocina back to the cave. Cocina called me on her cell phone, and said that she was going back to the cave with the man, and the woman would wait for me and guide me up. The couple said that we would probably need ropes and some first aid gear.

I called the Fire Department and they responded within 10 minutes with their rescue gear. Even the Boat Rescue Crew came in from the ocean side. Meanwhile, Cocina and the Japanese man arrived at the cave, and saw the boys bobbing up and down in the water below. The water was its highest peak, and it looked like only twenty to thirty feet below the lip of the cave. They were extremely careful not to slide in like Derek had done. Cocina yelled down, "Stay strong boys. Dad is bringing the Fire Department and some ropes."

Anthony screamed, "Thanks, Mom. I don't know how much longer Derek can last. He is so tired from bouncing around, and swallowing water."

Cocina answered, "Hang on to each other. Keep hold of him. We're going to get you out of there." The Japanese man was also yelling encouragement in his own language.

Cocina glanced down the trail, and saw two firefighters running up the trail full blast, carrying ropes and some snorkeling gear. I was right behind them, but not able to keep up their pace. Carlos had heard about the boys from Lola and ran past me up the trail. We soon saw there was a problem in anchoring the ropes on top if we threw over a line and life preserver into the cave for flotation and rescue. There were no trees, or cars, or huge rocks to tie to on top. We also had the problem was trying not to slide in and changing roles from rescuers to cave victims.

Anthony yelled out, right after one of the tide surges, "Mom, I lost Derek somewhere. I can't find him!"

Before I could even reply, Carlos slipped by me, wearing his life vest and snorkeling gear, and jumped into the cave. He hit with a huge splash, and was soon diving, looking for Derek. It was almost dark in the cave, and he had to do his search by feel. Being an experienced islander, and reading the currents, he moved into the backwash area and dove again. In seconds, he was back on top of the water, holding Derek. The boy appeared lifeless. He applied mouth-to-mouth resuscitation. The boy spit out a large spray of water, and kept coughing and spitting out more water. The late evening light was almost gone. Carlos yelled up, "He'll make it. He's breathing."

The other firefighters had brought up huge lights which operated from batteries. They also brought up long stakes and a sledge hammer. The firefighters knocked the stakes deep into the soil and rock, tied on the rescue ropes, and threw the ropes down into the cave to Carlos. He applied a diaper knot harness to Anthony. We pulled him up, and the stakes held tight. Cocina took hold of Anthony, while we then worked at pulling up Derek. Carlos said the boy was very weak. He applied one diaper harness to Derek on one rope, while he wrapped the second rope around his waist, and we pulled the two up together.

The paramedics went to work on both boys, and found only minor scratches and bruises. Lola had brought up some food and water, and the boys were soon nourished. Derek's eyes focused and his breathing stabilized and he was able to walk back to the hotel under his own power. As we traipsed back to the hotel, carrying

Continuin' On

rescue gear and just being happy and carefree, the evening sunset was a perfect blending of pink and blue, and re-assured us that we had another magnificent day coming our way in paradise. The air was soft, so tropical.

The Japanese couple joined us for a special lunch the next day, before their departure back to Narita. Our Korean chef, Guangman, was glowing when the Japanese man said, "This is the best Japanese meal that we've ever had. *Arigatoo.*" Guangman almost popped the buttons on his white jacket.

We treated the firefighters to a barbeque on the following Sunday. But as luck would have it, and their profession dictates, as they were sitting down, they got a fire call to the other side of the island. Guangman made up some "take-out" boxes, and dropped off his special entrees at the Fire Station. He never got a report back from the firefighters. Just so you know, chefs expect to hear back on their creations.

Anthony had taken it upon himself to notify the Coastal Resources agency about the dangerous cave. He guided the inspector up the hill to the cave, but since it was on public property, it was written off "a natural phenomenon." No danger notices were posted. However, we did prepare warnings for all our guests and hikers using the beach trail. Carlos took a long series of photos, and left them on the hotel bulletin board for the guests and workers to review before any hiking.

Better safe than sorry.

4

THE MAVEN PAYS A VISIT

We've all heard of *mavens*. It's a Yiddish-Hebrew term. They're not warlocks, ghosts, sorcerers, or evil spirits, or anything like that. They are experts in many things, and connoisseurs of cuisine and fine wines. The journalist and presidential speech writer, William Safire, made the term famous in the 1980's, when he referred to himself as a maven. They tend to look into the future and watch for societal trends. They are people of ideas, always observing and thinking.

I had worked with mavens of a sort, when I was a patrol sergeant in the high-crime areas of Los Angeles. These guys and gals knew the specific streets, the names of the gangs and their leaders, the best body armor to wear, the socio-economic structure of the neighborhood, the velocity of bullets, and who to see to get things done. They talk to a lot of people, read government reports and magazines, and generally get excited about any type of information.

One of my old police friends told me that Eric Schroeder, a retired deputy sheriff, was coming out to the hotel to check

Continuin' On

in with George and Jo about their Marriage Matchmaker business. Apparently Eric saw this as a great opportunity to find a beautiful, suitable wife, and if the business was sound, to expand it even further through his knowledge and contacts. Eric was a maven of the highest level. I knew him well. I had tried my best to supervise him and to turn him a productive cop. He never got past average. He wasn't a slacker but could best be described as distracted from the cop's real missions.

Eric was a knowledgeable, fun guy to find in a pub, or a think tank. He would be best described as a nerd. Some of his ramblings often seemed to me like an overdose of a thesaurus-type gobbledygook. He finally found his niche in Los Angeles when he was transferred to the Headquarters Research and Development Section. He was intelligent, personable and friendly. He was always reading newspapers, watching television documentaries, and doing a lot of comparisons about the best car to buy or where to take the 'best bang for your buck" vacation. The internet was a godsend developing his expertise and interests even further. I liked him, but had to be prepared for a long detailed talk about minutiae. I once asked why NASA was located in Florida and Texas, and after about an hour, I signaled for a friend to call me on the phone for a bogus emergency.

George was also a retired deputy sheriff, and had known Eric in East Los Angeles. He knew that Eric was not a hard-charger, a typical strong working cop. He wasn't thrilled about the visit, but figured since Jo did most of the business transactions of their matchmaking, that he would turn Eric over to Jo to find a possible bride and for his ideas on expansion. Jo had talked about opening a China office, so the timing was perfect. She figured that most of the brides were Chinese, and the grooms were Americans, why not expand to China. I told George that Eric would be the guy to do a cost analysis, and would evaluate the chances for a profitable outcome. Knowing Eric, he would find a way to make the ever-changing US immigration work for the business.

Eric arrived a few weeks later. He had six suitcases with him, and said that he planned on staying for a few months. Cocina set him up with a nice room on the fifth floor with a beach view and with a soft breeze right off the mountains, and with wireless internet. Eric looked in good shape and his belly was still flat. I told him to keep trying on his sheriff's uniform to remind himself not get too lazy about working out and staying fit. He grinned and said that he had some special plans about staying in shape and wanted George to find him a young, energetic sexual partner.

He met with George and Jo the next day, and agreed to participate in the "fast-date program" in the evening. Thirty single Chinese and Filipina ladies would be meeting thirty eligible American and Japanese men for possible love mates. The Filipinas spoke English, but most of the Chinese ladies would need friends to help them translate the conversation. Carlos' wife, Daisy, would coordinate the translators, and help out where needed. She also arranged for language lessons at the hotel for the men and women. Our in-house maven Eric downloaded simple, conversationalist language lessons for all the participants from the internet.

Eric went shopping and was soon decked out in aloha shirts, flip-flops and surfer shorts. I gave him a quick visit and the tourist introduction to Saipan. Of course, he had done his research, and knew where the World War II invasion beaches were, the casualties on both sides, the type of weapons used, and all about Guy

Continuin' On

Gabaldon, The Pied Piper, the hero marine from East Los Angeles. Eric said that Guy deserved the Medal of Honor, and I agreed.

I asked, "Are you ready for your dating round table tonight?"

"I am. I talked to George already. He says that over 175 couples have been matched up and married. As far as he knows, the couples are still together, but the immigration into the US is a big hassle. No problem getting into Saipan with its own immigration system. There's a huge logjam, at the US Immigration Division with the illegal border jumpers from Mexico. And China is still is still a communist country, so US Immigration authorities are extra careful about the Chinese immigrants."

I asked, "But what do you think about George and Jo's round robin?"

He said, "Good. Most people can make up their minds about some one in a matter of minutes. It doesn't take forever to see if you are attracted to that person."

"George only allows ten minutes per station. He rings a bell and you move onto the next station. What can you learn about someone in just a few minutes?"

"Think back to our computer scenario training in "shoot – don't shoot." We made decisions in fractions of seconds, based on our knowledge and experience. No reason we can't do it with romance."

"Yeah, you may be right. Better head over that way to the big conference room."

George and Jo had organized the room so that thirty ladies had their own number and table around the big room, number one to thirty. There was a chair in front of the table for the man. The men were numbered one to thirty with a tag on their shirts. Jo explained the fast-date and how it would work. Number one man would start with number 1 woman and talk to her for ten minutes. She could have her translator with her if she needed one. Daisy explained the rules to the Chinese ladies in Mandarin. The Filipinas agreed that they knew enough to carry on a conversation without a translator. The schools in the Philippines start the children out in English in the first grade. Then after the ten minute reminder, the men would rotate to the next table. Both sides of the conversations could make notes, and also arrange with George and Jo to meet the next day, if one of the match-ups looked promising.

At the end of the evening, our candidate Maven found four likely matches for him. Unfortunately only two of the ladies felt that way in their notes. Both of the possible match-ups were Chinese, and one spoke rudimentary English and had been a business woman in Canton. Eric found her promising, and made an appointment to talk the next day.

Over a late dinner, he spoke to George and Jo about possible plans of expanding to China. He had read about the political and economic situation in China, and had researched immigration policies. He was willing to obtain a business visa to China, and start up a satellite office, if it worked out with the Chinese woman, Wong Haiao.

Eric and Wong met the next day for lunch. Guangman was a sucker for romance, and fixed up a special meal, complete with flowers and herbs from Yoshi's garden. The Beachologist, Fred Cannon, and a few of his buddies came by and played some soft ukulele music. The couple felt the instant sparks, and after their meal, took a walk on the beach with their liqueurs. They sat under a palm tree for two hours, gesturing and eventually holding hands.

Continuin' On

Two days of more talking and hugging, led to a long night of romance. After four days, Wong gave up her room and moved in with Eric. We never saw them for the next five days. Room service was very busy. Occasionally they would call down for clean sheets and towels, and while the housekeeping crew was busy, they would sit out on their porch and soak up rays. Right on cue with her American slang, Cocina called their room "the cocoon of love" and predicted that "happy butterflies" would soon emerge.

On the fifth day of hibernation, Eric took his laptop to the business office, and printed out his business plan for George and Jo. There was a section devoted to evaluating the applicants for the sincerity of their intentions. Eric was very careful not to turn the operation into a sex tour of China.

George and Jo liked the plan, not only the input from Eric but soon saw that Wong knew what she was doing with profits and expenses. Eric had not only found a love-mate, but also another maven, Asian-style. Casually, Eric asked, "Oh yeah. We want to get married here on Saipan, USA. Should I research the process or can you help?"

George grinned and said, "I think we can assist you there. We've had plenty of practice, almost two hundred marriages so far. In fact, out of your fast-date group four Filipina and eight Chinese ladies found the right husbands. All Americans except for one Japanese man."

Eric and Wong were married in a simple ceremony on the beach. The mayor did the service and joined the wedding party for the traditional island buffet of barbeque, red rice, plenty of veggies and fresh fruit. Of course, we had a few hula dancers, and guitar and ukulele music.

Eric sent for his Chinese visa from Los Angeles, and two weeks later the couple was on their way to Canton. Wong had already arranged for several offices to evaluate, and had contacted advertising agencies for publicizing their new business. She knew all about obtaining business licenses and paying taxes in China, or making payments on an informal basis to make things move faster.

Our visiting maven had met a Chinese maven. Would they be competitive and try to out-think, out-read, and out-perform each other? Or would there be a synergetic effect? Wong wanted to have a child, and would the child be born on a precise day, at a certain weight and length, have a predicted life expectancy, and would the IQ level already be determined at conception? What would be the best sexual position for a quick pregnancy? Would they determine the child's gender by evaluating genes on certain days and room temperature? Plenty for them to think about.

The business in Canton took off like gangbusters. Eric and Wong soon found themselves hiring new helpers and looking for a larger office. Never a dull moment for a maven.

5

GOT BETEL NUT?

                    Islanders are wonderful, outgoing people. Mainlanders love their music and legends, and their strong, handsome features. Most of them are a mixture of past colonial powers, such as Spain, Germany, and Japan, combined with Korean, Chinese, Filipino and Bangladeshi influences. America came along after World War II, with their "melting pot" backgrounds, and they too, blended with the local peoples. Today, finding a so-called pure Chamorro or Carolinian is highly unlikely.

    Oftentimes, the local people are sedated or stimulated, depending on their companions or time of day, with a variety of substances. The outside influences brought along beer and spirits called "hot stuff," and tobacco. Members of the Peace Corps allegedly introduced marijuana from seeds harvested on the big island of Hawaii. Japan is a supplier of amphetamines "ice" to the islands. Local intoxicants include the harvesting and fermenting of coconut blooms for *tuba*, and the planting of *sakau* root to make *kava*. Pohnpei is a nearby island, and has the only known flag on the planet that has a picture of a bowl of an intoxicant, sakau, on its flag. All of these non-nutritional substances, of course, contribute to a high level of abuse, heart disease, diabetes and obesity. The CNMI has one of the highest per capita incidences of diabetes in the entire world.

But the biggest offender of all in the drug field is the simple little betel nut (areca catecha). People chew the nut at the beach, on their jobs, and in church. It has many names such as *tamul, pinang, areca, buyo* and is known locally as *pugua-ugam*. It is mildly stimulating, and releases a high level of psychoactive alkaloids, and compares to nicotine in its mind-altering powers. It has been around a long time. Jesuit Priest Peter Coomans discussed it in one of his journals about local Chamorros using betel nut in 1668.

Preparation of the betel nut takes time, and is often a social event. Users carry a woven basket, and they swap back and forth the ingredients used for the nut preparation, and like to talk about the strength and taste of the nuts from various islands and Asian countries. The nut grows on a tree from the palm family. The nut is cut up with a *sarota* knife into small pieces, covered with coral lime, and then wrapped up in a pepper leaf. Some users like to add cloves, ginger, whiskey or cigarettes for additional flavor. The chewing and spitting then begins. The user chews the nut for about twenty minutes to release all the chemicals. By this time, the mouth wad is bright red, and the user spits the spent nut out onto the ground, into the jungle or into a cup. Spitting also takes many art forms such as the V-shaped finger maneuver that does the trick of directing the steady flow for accuracy and distance.

The betel nut is occasionally used in ceremonies, and can be a symbol of friendship. It is not a controlled substance by law, either on the mainland or in the CNMI. However, one of the biggest problems is all the red spit on the sidewalks and buildings. It is so widely used on the Yap Islands, that many people call those islands, "The Land of the Vampires." A visitor can expect to find red stains on just about everything, including hotel walls and restaurant floors. The nut juice is also a carcinogen and can result in oral cancer. The lime and chemicals can burn a hole in the users' cheeks after a few years. In between all of that, the chewing leads to stained and broken teeth. Another problem is that employers lose valuable work hours, while their employees are using the nut and socializing, and are constantly under the influence of a stimulant.

This was happening at our Beach Hotel. I started noticing red stains on the parking lot and on the beach. The tourists were alarmed when they saw the stains, thinking it was dried blood. When they heard it was spit, they would crunch up their faces in disgust at such an unhealthy habit. I saw an eleven-year-old Palauan boy chewing by the pool. I noticed that some of our local employees were chewing nut, and that they were not our most productive team members. I knew something had to be done when I saw several of my Filipino workers chewing, including two ladies. The habit was spreading.

For the sake of good health and appearance, and not being bashful, I put out the order no more chewing betel nut on hotel premises or in hotel vehicles. The no-smoking rule was already in effect. Carlos told me that it was going to be tough going for several of the longtime betel nut users. Within days, the Filipinos and the ladies quit chewing, at least at work. Several of them were still coming to work with red-stained lips and teeth.

Three of the local men, all longtime chewers, were sneaking off the premises for a chew. They were caught by Mario II, our security chief, and given warnings. That was enough for one of the men, but the last two chewers kept sneaking away and not doing their jobs. Eventually Cocina had to fire them and send them on their way. They were both married with children and had to work to support their families. This filthy habit was contributing significantly and negatively to the community, comparing to gambling in societal disintegration.

It was a classic study in watching how people handle their problems. The older man, Pete, made it clear that if he wanted to chew betel nut, he would chew betel nut. He wasn't about to compromise or accept responsibility for his family or his own health. He found some family land, and planted two hundred betel nut trees. In the interim while they were growing (about 6 years to produce good nuts), he became a wholesaler in the nut business. Charley took a different route. He just floundered for several weeks, and kept borrowing nuts from other people.

Charley saw me in the Six Rounds Bar one afternoon having lunch. He walked over and yelled at me that I had really mucked-up his life. He knocked a water glass off the table, and challenged me to go outside. Several of the other bar patrons took hold of him, and pushed him away. Withdrawing from any drug is a bitch. The bar owner apologized and I finished my special meal of fresh tuna *sashimi* and *sushi*. Nothing should spoil a fresh seafood meal.

The next day, Carlos looked up from his desk at the PI office, and said, "You better look outside. Here comes Charley, the crazy guy." Charley was carrying a box of donuts. Carlos slid his baseball bat under his desk, saying, "Gotta be ready. The donuts

Continuin' On

might be a ploy to catch us off guard."

I laughed and said, "He's all of 150 pounds. Doesn't look real dangerous."

Charley walked into the office, and put the donuts on my desk. He meekly said, "Boss, I'm sorry. I wasn't myself yesterday. That was my third day without a nut, and I was feeling really weird. I blamed it all on you."

I said, "So, what's the deal? Why are you here?"

He said, "I was so embarrassed yesterday in front of all my friends. I had a long talk with my wife. I want to apologize, and let you know that I'm kicking the nut habit."

Carlos said, "You say that today. How about tomorrow?"

"I'm determined. No more nut. No more wasted money. No more broken teeth and cancer."

I said, "Charley, you go without nut for a month, I'll hire you back. But Carlos and I will watch your every move."

"Okay, I'll do it."

I gestured towards the main hotel office, and said, "I'll let Cocina know, and we expect a day's work out of you for a day's pay. Understand?"

He nodded in agreement, and left the office. I looked at Carlos, and asked, "Think he'll make it?"

Carlos replied, "He's got reason enough. We'll know in a month."

Meanwhile, the ugly red stains disappeared around the hotel, but were still evident in the public tourist areas and the community parks. I suppose a lot more have to die of cancer before the message is received loud and clear. And meanwhile, offend a few hundred more tourists.

One month to the day, Charley reported to work. There were

no signs of betel nut use. Cocina put him on the landscaping crew. The gardening supervisor, Yoshi, liked his energy. Charley brought in a few new native plants for Yoshi's gardens, which enriched the photos and drawings of the senior citizen gardening club. No one talked about betel nut trees.

6

THE ISLAND WET T-SHIRT CONTEST

One of the fun events twice a year at various island hotels is aptly called 'The Hooters Festival." It is just another name for a wet T-shirt contest, and the twin orbs of nurture are called heavenly bodies, tits, breasts, boobs, *susos,* bosoms, titties, hooters, udders, chichis, toddies, milk packs, *tetes,* or teats. The hooters event is rotated between hotels on a schedule sheet issued by the hotel association. The participants like to know the dates two months in advance, so they get physically fit in time, or make a trip to the Philippines for a breast enhancement operation. Because of the stigma attached to such a celebration in some quarters, especially the vocal feminists, about half the hotels don't participate. The Beach Hotel's turn came up for the first time for the spring dates.

It was time to talk it over with Cocina, being the hotel manager and more importantly, my wife. I was the mere owner, and knew that it never makes sense to aggravate one's wife, or even some of my female staff, like Myla and Aubrey at the front desk, or Lola on the beach, or Masako, our language teacher.

Some women find such events to be demeaning, and in addition, most Asian women are not as naturally endowed as European and American women. Their breasts are functional and beautiful, but not magnificently designed to attract the male animal. The Russians are our latest guests, escaping from the Siberian winters. They stretch the bras to double E without any trips to the plastic surgeon.

Much to my surprise, Cocina said, "You are a bad man, but what the hell, it sounds like a good idea. Give me some time to talk it over with the girls." She came back to me about two hours later, and said, "It's a go. In fact, Myla wants to participate and also another large-busted Filipina called Joyful." Carlos overheard the conversation and immediately volunteered to be a judge. We set the first place prize at $500, followed by $300, and $200. Fourth and fifth prize winners would get a $100 prize each.

The boys at the hotel had heard the rumors about the contest, and once it got out that Cocina had approved, they were soon offering to work the event without pay. One of the local guys said that his wife had just graduated from ballet class, and wanted to be one of the contestants. Mario II volunteered to be the water boy, that's the worker that "wets and waters" the girls. I supposed such a chore would fall under his work specifications as maintenance supervisor.

I spoke to Myla later at the front desk. I said, "Hey M, you surprised me by going in the contest."

"Whatsa mean, Boss-man. You don't think I qualify?"

I gave a little stammer and said, "Oh yeah, you qualify. No doubt there. So why do you want to do it?"

"It suits my personality. I'm an extrovert and a little rebellious against society's rules. I like being hot and the center of attention.

Continuin' On

It's okay with my husband."

I said, "The feminists think you might develop low self-esteem, eating disorders and depression. Some even think you're just being used by men as a sexual object."

"In some cases that might be true. No one is forcing me to do the show. I want to do it and have fun. I like to dance and be free. If I don't win, no big deal. I know my sweet husband will be there cheering me on, and taking me home."

I answered, "Well, you have fun. Struggle on, Sister. I've got to get back to work and get the crews moving."

Beachologist Fred needed some part-time work, so I put him in charge of designing a stage near the high tide line, where the girls could strut and dance. I wanted the wet T-shirt area to be away from the main courtyard of the hotel, and laid out to irritate the least amount of guests. I also offered to move the guests to a friend's nearby hotel if they felt offended. One of our older Japanese guests, Noriko, didn't want to move. He said in broken English, "Me, I wanna see. I like lady's tits." His wife Asako, joined in and said, "I wanna see what I used to look like. I all fall down now."

Guangman built his buffet table and bar in close proximity to the stage. Mario II got all the speakers and lights installed. I hired a local DJ named Dirty Luke to do the music and lighting arrangement. He had done this before at other hotels, and according to our steady partygoers, the fun and excitement never slowed down for four hours. There are no disturbance and noise laws on the island but I made sure that I invited my neighbors, and promised to shut everything down right after midnight. Lola made assignments to her crew with specific instructions to leave the beach cleaner than when the first Spanish explorers arrived.

I had never organized a wet T-shirt contest before. I had been a judge several times. It gets crazy when you pick the wrong girl, and her boyfriend gets upset and actually pushes you in the chest before security can haul him away. That happened to me in New Jersey; so for our island event, there would be plenty of security officers available. I made sure there were female officers aboard, because again in New Jersey, two lady contestants were scratching and biting in a catfight, when one of the ladies thought she was being upstaged by the other gal with smaller breasts. It's not a matter of prize money, but who has the nicest, sought-after rack; and who can drive the lads over the top.

Cocina had special white T-shirts made up with the hotel logo. She wore one in the ocean one evening, and her gorgeous brown breasts showed through the material quite nicely. Being mammals, we had to imitate the other ocean mammals, and prove quite emotionally and scientifically that love and lust can be accommodated underwater and on top of the water. Cocina in her usual American slang said, "Now, that's what I call waterworks. No wonder seals always sound so happy when they're barking away." I was in a hurry to finish. I knew sunset was feeding time for the sharks, and wasn't enthusiastic about losing part of my dangling anatomy.

Aubrey knew all the PR people in town. She had flyers printed and placed in all the bars. She did the radio spots, and appeared on television a dozen times in her well-known yellow bikini. She was an advertisement for the hotel all by herself. What a gorgeous attraction. The big night was fast-approaching, and we now had twenty contestants. Each girl had to sign a liability waiver form, and submit a one dollar entry fee. She had to acknowledge that she was entering a wet T-shirt contest and that she would be sprayed with water and subjected to a lot of yelling from quasi-crazed males.

The contest was set for Saturday night. We did a walk-through rehearsal on Friday, and actually had several of the volunteer female staff wearing the white T-shirts and being sprayed by Mario II. He grinned and said, "Boss, I'm just doing my job. Gotta rehearse you know. Gotta get it right." After this practice session, I noticed several couples wandering off into the jungle. It's always hot in the tropics.

Dirty Luke got all his DJ gear set up and offered a few insights into lighting and the choreography. It was Aubrey's job to keep the stage under control, and the contestants moving. It was purposeful, planned chaos, ready to erupt.

As the clock struck eight on event night, we had a line of several hundred guys and about fifty curious females, mostly sans bras. It would be a profitable and memorable evening. Security checked their ID's and made sure we didn't have any underage people sneaking in, especially from the beach side. The island motorcycle gang, the Taga Beach-Runners, showed up and offered to help hotel security if there were problems. Most the guys, and some of their mamas, were decked out in leathers and chains, and covered with tattoos. It was tough to believe that about half of them were businessmen and government workers. Their leader looked like Man Mountain Dean on steroids.

Twenty-two contestants finally entered. The evening started with dancing, singing and socializing on the sand. Dirty Luke had picked the right music, loud and raucous, to get everyone warmed up and ready for fun. He liked to yell between songs, "Hey, it's time for rock and roll. It's almost *suso* time. Ladies, shake those bosoms." Some of the lady dancers didn't wait for suso time, and were already raising their blouses.

Plastic bead necklaces went on sale for a buck apiece. The lads were intending to be busy anointing their favorites with special attention. Ivan Royal laid down a *Ben Franklin*, and walked away with a hundred necklaces. He would get a lot of attention.

We had three judges, Carlos being the Supreme Judge. Two local business men had volunteered to be Associate Judges, Jaime Bonaventura and Wong Wai. The girls would be judged on how many beads they were given from the audience, dancing skills, strutting ability with fully extended breasts, gyrating antics and showmanship, and general poise. Each of the five categories would be worth ten points for a total of fifty points, and then this was doubled for the final percentage. The top five contestants would repeat their performance, and then do a group dance for the finale.

I asked Cocina how things were going. She answered, "Just fine, Tom-cat. Guangman is doing a great business with his bar and buffet. The admission fee from the guys will give us the money to pay a nice bonus to the so-called hotel worker "volunteers." And I notice most of your ladies are here."

I laughed and said, "You bad girl. These are not all my ladies, only a few."

"I might have to go to the P.I. for some "uplifting" suso work. Whatsa think?"

This was definitely a loaded question. There was only one answer. "Baby, you are beautiful just the way you are. And besides, you have the world's best butt."

She said, smiling, "Yeah, that's true." I did a drum roll with my fingers on the counter, and she shook her little butt.

I asked, "How are our hotel guests doing?"

Continuin' On

She answered. "This may surprise you. No one was offended and no one checked into the other hotel. I offered them free room service. The families are just staying in their rooms, or going to the movie theatre. And if you look close at our beach crowd, there are about twenty Korean and Japanese couples that have joined in the fun. Noriko and Asako are right in the middle of the dancing crowd. Asako isn't wearing a bra."

The strutting and fun started right at nine o'clock. The music was loud, and the beer was flowing. No bras allowed on stage. We had most of the island populations represented, starting with two Korean and one Japanese girl who had visited the plastic surgeon. Four Filipinas had apparently had the same doctor. Myla did her walk on stage, and being completely natural, the lads loved it. The three blonde Russian girls were instant hits. The local ballet dancer in her tutu with her bright red thong panties, and a very wet T-shirt, brought thundering applause. Another attention-getter was a Chinese gal who displayed incredible courage, and did her strut with a typical Asian 32A size. A Bangladeshi girl came out on stage with a shiny gold skirt and a T-shirt. The remaining girls were typical island combos of local and Spanish, and locals and mainland American. All beautiful women.

Aubrey directed the girls do their strut, wearing whatever they wanted. Most of them were wearing bikini bottoms and the white T-shirt. She attached a number to the bottom garment, so the judges knew the girls' identities. On the next strut, Mario II worked them over his water-hose, and now the gals were wet, and the crowd was going wild. Dirty Luke would announce the girl's name, and off she would go. Depending how badly she wanted the attention and the win, she'd dance to the audience at stage edge and bend her head for a pearl necklace. If she got ten, she would have full points in that category. They all eye-balled Ivan Royal with his box of one hundred necklaces. Some of the girls yelled out that they were thirsty, and the lads would shake up their beer or soda cans, and she would move in for a liquid bath.

On the third strut, the girls were welcome to improvise and improve any of their scores with showmanship. Some tore their T-shirts to shreds, revealing their breasts to remarkable sensuality. Some made sexually suggestive moves with their bodies, especially their mouths and butts. Others placed ice cubes on their nipples to make them stand proud and straight. By this time, just about every girl had at least ten beads and full points. One of the Russian girls and the Chinese girl had over twenty necklaces each.

After the third strut, Dirty Luke slowed down the music and softened the lights. The judges were busily making their decision of the Top Five. The contestants had come off the stage and were mingling with the crowd. Some hadn't bothered covering up.

During the break, I noticed three local jerks looking over at Cocina's sister, Dina Miradora. She was wearing her bra and a green blouse, and was wearing shorty-shorts. She wasn't being flamboyant or trying to attract attention to herself. The jerks kept watching her, then whispering to one another. One of the jerks pretended he was humping her. She was completely unaware, and just having a good time with her friends. I gestured over to Dina and told her to stand with me. I asked Carlos who the three jerks were. He said, "They're bad news, total assholes. All three of them have been busted. The big guy is Juan Riviera and the real fat dude is Jack Fernandez. They're the guys that raped Mei and got released. The other guy is Richardo Zambales. He's into everything illegal and violent, including dope and child

Continuin' On

molestation. Zambales would fuck a snake if he could get it to stay still."

There was a loud electronic rapping of cymbals from Dirty Luke, and we looked up to the stage. Dina went back to her friends. The jerks drifted into the crowd. I never saw them again.

Aubrey yelled out, "Are you ready for the winners?" The crowd yelled back, "Hell, ya!" She announced the Top Five winners, slowly and deliberately. These five would do another strut and dance, and then they would be placed in order. She gave out the names: Miki, the Japanese; Myla, the Filipina; Cheyanne, the Chamorro ballet dancer; Kai, the Chinese; and Magdalena, the Russian. If I hadn't seen the great dancing and strutting, I would guessed that the judges were trying to be politically correct and not offend anyone. But that wasn't the case. These gals could strut their stuff and were fantastic entertainers.

All five stayed on the stage and did their routines. Mario II watered them down again. The other contestants were cheering them on. All the girls were into it. At one time, I counted about thirty sets of bare breasts dancing and bobbing in the audience. Cocina saw me counting mentally, and gave me one of her little sexy, know-all smiles.

Aubrey made the winning announcements. Cheyanne and Miki won the fourth and fifth spots respectively. Number three was Myla and the second prize went to Magdalena. To most everyone's surprise, first place went to Kai, the little Chinese. She scored a ten in every category, and the judges gave her a ten point bonus for her seductive dancing, and for her courage in walking on stage with all the full-bosomed ladies.

Even though there had been a lot of drinking, there were no fights, and no one got pissed off at the judges' decisions. The event had just thirty minutes before closing time, and Guangman rang the bell for last call. I noticed Daisy walking over to Carlos. She said, "Time to come home, big hombre. I know you have a thing for Chinese girls."

He said, "Kai won fair and square. She's one hell of a dancer and can really shake her booty."

"Well, let her shake her booty for someone else. I've got a cool bottle of chardonnay waiting for us."

Carlos looked over at me and said, "I'm heading home. Don't worry about the hotel rocking and shaking. It's just us doing several levels of booty research. Might make the scientific journals."

Cocina strolled over and waved at Carlos and Daisy, arm in arm. She said, "They look like a couple in love."

I said, "Yeah but nothing like our love—ours is written in the stars."

She said, "You been drinking or smoking?"

I said, "I'm drunk on love. You're my intoxicant, *mi corazon*."

She laughed and lightly punched me on the shoulder. It had been a good night. I thought about all the fun and excitement that we had created for people, our friends and guests. And I thought about Chinese Kai who was strong and confident in herself and her body, and happy about whom she was. She deserved the bonus points.

I still had an uneasy feeling about the three jerks in the audience. Noriko walked past me and said, "Arigatoo, Tom. We had good time." Asako was hanging on his arm.

I shook his hand and said goodnight. I made sure Dina got home okay. It was a long way from the violent streets of South Central LA, but we still had to maintain our vigilance for the goddamn predators lurking in the shadows.

7

FALSE SELLING TO YAKUZA

Little Jimmy Reyes had made a fairly good living for himself and his family since he was fourteen years old. He sold tangan-tangan leaves, sometimes missed in with oregano, to the tourists as "maui-wowee" in baggies that gradually increased in price to twenty-five dollars for a small baggie. He dried the leaves and herbs, crushed them into nondescript pieces, and told the tourists how to roll the cigarettes, and sometimes even gave them rolling papers for good measure. He knew that good selling includes timing and packaging, and he had picked up skills along the way of pulling his customers into a dark alley. He would then look over his shoulder and pretend that he was on the look-out for undercover narcotics officers.

Jimmy had an important secret from his cousin at the police station. When the undercover guys did go to work, Jimmy knew about it before the officers left the station. Even if they were working, he had very little concern because they could screw up even a slam-dunk caper. They knew shit about search and seizure court decisions.

The tourists didn't know the laws either or the local routines. With his big brown-eyes, Jimmy was a great actor in working out the possibility of him, and the tourists, being arrested. He told them not to tell anyone, especially hotel security, because the charge would result in jail time, and a story in the newspaper. Sometimes his clients were so pleased with the deal and his concern, that they would give him a five or a ten dollar tip. Occasionally they over-tipped in *yen*. It was an exciting part of their island trip.

Jimmy and his friends would often have a good laugh afterwards about his customers trying to light up a tangan-tangan cigarette. The leaves burn very quickly, almost like a flash, and not slow like tobacco or marijuana. Most of his clients were Japanese, and if they were defrauded, they would take the deception in stride, and would never think about making a complaint. Marijuana is a big deal in Japan. They had no idea that possession of marijuana is only an infraction in most US states, and not something to be alarmed about.

But Jimmy knew, that under island law, a sale of narcotics was a felony, if the substance was purported to be marijuana, even if the leaves were tangan-tangan. If he made a series of sales in the Garapan tourist area, he would stay away for several days. By then, many of his clients would have returned home. The clients that he did see, mostly ignored him, but some actually said that the tangan-tangan leaves gave them a high. Suggestive behavior, along with alcohol, will often give a buzz. In his illegal career, Jimmy had made several repeat sales to customers that enjoyed the tangan-tangan leaves. He would smile, and take their money.

Eventually criminals screw up, and Jimmy did it in a big way.

Continuin' On

One evening, Jimmy saw two husky Japanese men coming in his direction. He didn't notice that the men were covered with tattoos, and had missing fingers, both being symbols of the organized crime group in Japan, the Yakuza. Jimmy did his spiel, and gave four baggies to the two men. They said that they were getting some "weed' for their boss. The men didn't reach for their money. Jimmy had no idea that the Yakuza were often "comped" for their hotel rooms, car rentals, prosties, and food wherever they went.

Jimmy said, "Hey man, where's my hundred bucks? How about some yen?"

The older Japanese man said, "Hey, it's for the boss."

"I don't care who it's for. Give me my money."

The other Japanese said, "This stuff doesn't look right. Not the right smells either."

Jimmy said, "It's different texture here, man, and it's stronger than Hawaii."

The men said, in Japanese, that translated to, "Fuck off little man. Get lost." They turned and walked away.

Jimmy had never had this happen. The men were too ominous to tackle, and he couldn't afford a hassle with the police. He was the one breaking the law. He let them walk away and wrote it off part of the game. He was determined to make it up on the next customers. He knew by experience that the younger tourists wanted to try marijuana, especially the naïve girls. He was particularly adroit at fast-changing and confusing the timid Japanese female tourists. No problem for Jimmy. He made up the lost money in several hours.

For the next few days, he stayed out of Garapan and away from tourists. He lost several hundred dollars at the poker machines in his village, and decided it was time to go back to work. Within an hour back on the streets, he was approached by two pimps who told him that some Japanese guys were looking for him. Jimmy believed this was good news. He was always willing to supply what they wanted. Sometimes they left a cell-phone number, but not in this case. Jimmy would have to watch for them.

The Yakuza men found him first. He didn't see them until it was too late. They pulled him into an alley, and dropped him to his knees with several shots to the solar plexus. An old Chinese man exited the back of his restaurant into the alley, and saw the Yakuza, and ran back into the restaurant. He didn't call 911.

The older Japanese man spoke enough English to relay that they were extremely angry about the phony marijuana, and that their boss had slapped them, and took $500 out of their pay. He said, "Regeno, fake marijuana! We want real ganja."

As Jimmy began to stand up, the younger Japanese man dropped him again with a hard slap to the back of his head. Jimmy still had no idea about the history of the Yakuza, but he sensed he was in big trouble. He told them he would get what ever they needed. The men stripped off his watch and rings, and took his wallet. He was down to only twenty dollars but they found his driver license with his home address, and all the phone numbers for the family members.

The older man told him to call his friends and relatives, and get some real marijuana down to the alley, or he would die. The older man said that Jimmy didn't get the weed fast, he would kill five family members, one by one. Jimmy believed these guys. He called his first marijuana source, and no answer. He was sweating, and his stomach was churning. Jimmy felt like he was ready to lose his last meal.

Jimmy made three calls before he made a connection to a

Continuin' On

farmer high in the mountains. He told his source that he wanted a full kilo, and pronto. The farmer asked for money, and Jimmy said that he was short, but would sign over his Toyota pickup, and then when he got paid for the marijuana, he'd make the payment with interest.

Within an hour, the farmer showed up in the alley behind the donut shop. Jimmy walked out from the shadows, and handed his keys over. The farmer saw the Japanese men in the alley, and asked who they were.

Jimmy said, "Just customers. That's all you need to know. Now, get out of here. Don't look back"

Jimmy saw his pickup zoom off, driven by the farmer's son. He walked back into the alley, and gave the kilo to the older man.

The older Japanese man said to his cohort, "Should we kill this guy, or just cut off his ears?" Jimmy understood that part, but they switched to Japanese.

While Jimmy was still trying to sort out the language, the younger man slipped behind him, and snapped his right arm at the elbow. While Jimmy was screaming in pain, the older man took his left arm and broke it at the elbow with a sharp twist and judo chop.

All the restaurants and stores along the alley were owned by Asian businessmen. The commotion and screaming never prompted a call to the police or fire departments. The Yakuza men casually started back to their hotel, nodding at several of the store owners. A short conversation took place with a pimp on the corner, and three beautiful Chinese ladies emerged from the next alley, and joined the two men on the short walk to their hotel.

The older man said in Japanese, "We'll let the boss have first choice."

"The way the boss is pissed off, we might just end with sloppy seconds on all three," said the other man.

Jimmy Reyes came to the International Private Investigations office the next day in a taxi. Both his arms were in casts. He told us his ludicrous story. He asked confidentially if there was anything that he could do about the two Japanese men. He also wanted his truck back from the marijuana farmer.

Carlos said, "You are one stupid son-of-a bitch. You're lucky to be alive." Carlos explained who the Yakuza were, kind of an Asian copycat of the Italian Mafia.

I said, "Forget about your truck. It's gone, and be thinking about a new occupation. Maybe get an education and a job. The Feds are bringing in new agents from California, and working some of these undercover drug-buys, so you'll be out of business in Garapan." Stretching the truth about the long arms of Federal law often causes a little paranoia for the criminal mind.

Jimmy looked sad and downcast. Carlos added, "And by the way, your cousin got busted at the police station. The commissioner not only fired him, but also threw him in the jailhouse for a pile of misdemeanors. So your snitch contact is gone."

We weren't sure if his injuries and near-death experience made him depressed, or more likely the prospect of having a regular job. Jimmy left our office, shoulders downcast, no money, and hoping a friend or relative would give him a ride home.

8

SAILING WITH THE AUSSIES

The hotel lucked out when Herb and Lynda Carson sailed into Saipan on their forty-one foot, thirteen foot beam ketch. Their boat was aptly named *Ocean Freedom*. It was a light pastel green with a main mast and the back mizzen, and sails, pure white. They had been out to sea for about nine months, and had sailed into Tahiti from Australia, then Kosrae and Pohnpei, and made it north to our island. They were on their way to Japan, where they hoped to sell their boat and fly home to Melbourne. They were both health professionals, and had decided to take off a year while in their primo years. They were clearly adventurous souls. Herb had hand-painted "Aspire to inspire before you expire" on their bedroom wall below decks.

Once safely anchored in Smiling Bay Cove, they unloaded their motorcycle and off they went to explore Saipan. They liked our rose-colored hotel, sitting right next to the beautiful sandy beach, and decided to give the restaurant a try. Of course, Guangman heard the Aussie accent, and produced an excellent meal of lamb, potatoes and mint sauce. He told them to come back later for his magical pavlova pudding, made of light and fluffy meringue, and decorated with fresh fruit and whipped cream. Guangman even knew that the pudding was named after ballet dancer Anna Pavlova. It was interesting to watch Guangman explain to Australians that the special dessert is equally claimed by New Zealand and Australia as their original creation.

The couple contacted Myla at the desk and booked in for a week. They asked for a mountain view room, saying that they had seen enough of the ocean for awhile. They made a market run, and filled their little fridge with beer and more beer. Saipan has several liquor stores and they found their beloved Foster's and Victoria Bitter.

After they had settled in for a few days, Herb came to the PI office, and asked if there were back country trails for motorcycles. I took out the topographical map, and studied some of the old cattle and walking trails, and also some of the roads and railway lines that were developed in Japanese times for the sugar plantations, and for the Japanese Imperial Army.

He said, "Can you get a motorcycle? Let's take a ride. Get Cocina to ride with you. Lynda will be riding with me."

Carlos answered first, "I've got a bike. And Daisy loves to ride. I can get Tom a bike from a friend."

I said, "Let's do it. Cocina had been wanting to go in the back country. Tomorrow about eight o-clock in the morning?'

Carlos said, "There's a storm coming in, but so what. It'll be cool for the ride. Maybe we'll get in some mud-riding back in the hills."

The next day it rained like the heavens decided to irrigate the island all in one day. We rode along the mountain ridges,

Continuin' On

and stayed out of the mud most of the time, except when we crossed over a valley. The ladies looked like they had taken their morning showers fully dressed. They were all so beautiful with their stringy hair and their nipples standing proud through their shirts. Carlos just keep grinning, and said, "Now you boys know why I like taking the ladies on rainy rides?" Cocina and Lynda threw out their chests even further, while little Daisy crossed her arms over her breasts. Her face turned bright red.

We saw that both Herb and Lynda were excellent riders, and would often do acrobatic moves on their bike like the passenger going over the rider's head, and becoming the operator. Lynda was also smooth at riding Herb piggy-back, and also riding on his shoulders. These two were without fear. They never slowed down, and kept blasting through rain and mud, and jumping over fallen logs. They were wearing only shorts, tank tops, and flip-flops. The rest of our "motorcycle gang" felt like nerds and amateurs wearing helmets and leather boots.

It was one great experience. We got back to the hotel six hours later, and headed for the car wash area, where we had more fun with the hoses, spraying each other and intermittently washing the bikes. Cocina laughed so hard, she just collapsed and sat on her rump, while we sprayed her with three hoses. A classic day with a classic finish. There is no way to top such a satisfying, exciting day. But Guangman did his best by preparing and offering a Hawaiian luau, complete with ukulele music by my friend, the Beachologist.

Herb yelled out to Guangman, "Hey mate, *masarap and yo!*" He was adding new words to his vocabulary every day. Maybe take them home to Australia and use them along with dingo, billabong, barbie, waltzing Matilda, boomerang, and didgeridoo.

Lynda said, "Good on ya, mate."

Guangman nodded back and smiled. I knew from our past conversations that he only had the slightest idea what Herb and Lynda were saying with their Australian accents.

After the meal and music, Herb and Lynda left for a walk on the beach. They barely got past the restaurant light, when they dropped to the sand. It seemed, at least we were thinking vicariously, that nature was taking its course. Love is grand. It's always so hot in the tropics.

Herb and Lynda were preparing to leave in two days. We would miss their chatter, their insane stories, and their positive approach to every day. Herb said, "Look Tom, we have to take the Freedom out for a trial sail before we make the big run to Japan. We had some work done on the communications system, and on the mizzen sail. You and Cocina want to take a day trip with us? Maybe we could do some trolling on the way back."

I said, "Let me check with Cocina. Sometimes she gets a little seasick."

But Cocina showed no hesitation. She said that she was going to miss her new Aussie friends, and wanted to spend another day with them. She'd never met such brash, fearless, and confident people before. She added, "A fun-filled cruise with Herb and Lynda. How can I pass that up? *Fair dinkum*." Now my beautiful Cocina was into Australian slang.

We left at daybreak the next day. Guangman had prepared enough food for about twenty people. He included breakfast, as well as lunch. Herb was already into the beer, saying "it's going to a long, dry day."

We cleared the harbor, and Herb had me take over the wheel. He was preparing the sails to take in more wind for speed.

Continuin' On

Cocina poured some coffee and came over and sat by me. Lynda came from below decks, completely naked, except for her deck shoes. I tried not to stare but her body was magnificent. I shook my head, trying to clear my vision. We looked towards the bow, and Herb was adjusting some ropes, completely naked also, with his "little soldier" and his balls hanging out.

Herb walked back and saw we were a bit shocked. He stood before us, wearing only his deck shoes, and said, "Oh, I guess we forgot to tell you. We always sail naked, and feel free like God's creatures were meant to be. That okay?"

Herb and Lynda's privates were right at eye level. Being a big, brave retired cop that I am, I muttered something unintelligible kind of like,"Yeah, it's your boat. If you don't mind us being here. Might take some adjustment on our part."

Lynda sat next to us, naked as the day she was born, and asked for coffee. I noticed that she carried a little towel with her, and used it to sit down on the dusty, hot fiberglass rails. I could well imagine that a burned bebe would be most unpleasant. Herb went forward again, and adjusted some lines. Lynda went to help. As she was bending over, Cocina said, "Watch out, buster. Your eyes will bulge out of your head."

"Oh yeah, little Miss Righteous. Like you weren't staring at his *chili* and those tanned buns."

Cocina smiled and said, "I hardly noticed. I was watching how he tied the ropes."

"Yeah, you have to control yourself. Stop staring so hard."

She said, "What's that 'hard' play on words. Are you trying to trap me? Besides I love my Honey-bear." She tongued my right ear.

The rest of the day went that way, with lots of fun banter and innuendo. Right after lunch, we noticed Herb and Lynda cuddling and kissing near the bow, and they excused themselves to go below. As they walked past us, Herb had a full erection. I swear I heard Cocina let out a breath of hot air that sounded like "wow-wee." She denied it.

Herb and Lynda appeared on deck abut forty minutes later, both smiling. Herb glanced at Cocina, and said, "Your turn. Lynda will take the wheel." Cocina winced and moved closer to me.

Herb chuckled and said, "Relax Cocina, I meant you and Tom."

Cocina got the message, and took me at the arm and pulled me towards the stairs leading below. The next hour was one of foggy, hot and wet, and surreal rolling and jumping and adjusting. Cocina climaxed five times, and when I erupted, it was like being a teenager in his first experience.

I said, "That was totally lewd and wicked. Must be Herb and Lynda's sexiness that got you going."

She said, 'You blockhead. It's the ocean air and the sense of freedom and being wild. I was only thinking of you and your hot chili of love. And your raging balls of fire. Yeah, baby!" I cherished her more every day, and loved the American expressions that she learned from television or in her books. We showered and went topside.

Herb and Lynda were wearing idiotic grins. They were still naked, with Lynda sitting with her legs open. She said, "The fresh air and naked bodies do it every time. Isn't it just too wonderful? Mother Nature at her finest."

We agreed. As we headed back to the harbor, it cooled off, and Herb and Lynda slipped on some sweat pants and flannel tops. We got the boat cleaned up and secured and headed off for the hotel, where Guangman was waiting with a luscious meal

Continuin' On

and another Pavlova pudding. And some cold Aussie beer. We reluctantly said our goodbyes at midnight.

Herb and Lynda were gone at daybreak. They promised to stay in touch, and they did. They got to Japan, and found a buyer. The last we heard, they had a few days left and flew to Bali. We didn't hear from them for several weeks. There are dozens of internet cafes in Bali, and they weren't answering their emails. We called Herb's father in Australia, and found out that they had both been victims of the Muslim terrorist bombings in the two Bali night clubs. Two hundred and two people were senselessly murdered, eighty-eight of them Australians. Because the bodies were unidentifiable and mutilated, the families had them cremated, and their ashes scattered back home at their favorite beach near Adelaide.

Cocina and I went to our beach, and raised our glasses to Herb and Lynda during a stunning sunset. We pictured them "talking story" with their friends in the Bali clubs, and laughing until their sides were ready to burst.

Always the question, why do bad things happen to good people? Herb and Lynda were two of the nicest, most exciting and loving people on the planet. They would never be biased against any religion or skin color on the earth. They were care-givers by profession.

Answer: because that's the way it is. So…appreciate and celebrate every day to the fullest. Hug your friends and kiss your children.

9

SWEPT OFF THE ROCKS

Amos Enriquez was a young man who liked to have expensive, nice things but wasn't very enthused about having a job. In fact, he was lazy and just wanted to chew betel nut and go fishing. When he was working, which was seldom, he managed to qualify for several credit cards. If his credit was in the pits, he would apply under his Chinese wife's name, Wei Sun, who worked two jobs and managed to pay her bills, and sometimes Amos paid the balances on his cards. It was a *pro quo quid* situation. Amos had a caring and employed wife, and sex whenever he wanted it. Wei had her green card and their new baby, and was able to support several family members in China. It wasn't romance and love. It was more of a pragmatic arrangement for both parties. Wei liked it when he went fishing or drinking with his friends. He wasn't there to pester her or mess up the house.

Over the weekend, Amos tried his luck on the high slippery rocks at Banzai Cliff near Marpi in Saipan. The fishing is usually excellent, and oftentimes, large schools of fish will

Continuin' On

ride the currents at the point. A storm came up in the afternoon, and fishermen like Amos usually just moved back into the caves or behind large abutments of limestone for protection from the weather. Sometimes they stayed out all night, so no one worried when they didn't return for several days.

This storm grew in intensity, nearly reaching typhoon conditions. Amos didn't move back off the high rocks in time, and a large wave swept him into the sea. He thrashed and struggled and finally got pulled down into an underwater grotto. When he surfaced, he was scratched and bruised but alive. It was a large cavern with no exits that he could see except back through the ocean. There was a small hole high in the cave letting in some air and light. Miraculously his cell phone was still intact wrapped in a plastic baggie inside his jacket and had a full battery charge. He also had his lunch and some fishing tackle. Amos saw that there were crabs and fish in the pool at the base of the cavern.

Amos climbed up to a ledge where it was dry and found driftwood to build a fire. He knew how to make a fire by rubbing sticks together, but there was no immediate reason for a fire. He wasn't cold and he could eat the fish raw. There was a trickling spring of fresh water. He felt no sense of danger or immediate reason to try and escape. The only option was to swim back through the underwater wall opening to the ocean. The water was calm inside the cave, so his resting spot on the ledge would be safe to relax and sleep.

Amos owed a lot of money to a lot of people. The collection agencies were after him, and he had three civil court cases pending. The more he considered being lost over the cliffs, he thought this would be his chance to disappear and be pronounced dead. People would believe his body was eaten by sharks. He would have to figure a way to get to Guam and away from Saipan. Wei's immigration status would be okay, as widows continue their legal status when the husband dies. There were several witnesses to his loss at sea, so the story could be believable.

He slept for two days. He did some fishing, and ate several small *atulai, tataga* and *mafute* fish and a few crabs. Most people would be bored by now, and try to figure a way out of the dilemma. But Amos was an expert at loafing and still wasn't anxious or worried. On the fourth day, he called Wei on his phone. She was upset and relieved at the same time. He told her what happened, and what his plans were. She didn't disagree. They both talked fast because of the battery charge, but Wei knew where extra batteries might be at home.

Wei said that the Police Rescue Team was calling off the search. Amos' family members had been out in their boats but were also giving up. The family was planning on having him pronounced dead and starting rosaries the next day. She said the family was organizing nine rosaries to be followed by nine more, symbolizing an actual burial at sea. Wei said that everyone had been kind to her. Amos' father knew about bankruptcies, and said that he would help her get rid of all the debts.

Amos knew about where he was in the cliff formations. He said that he would lash together some branches and driftwood, and poke them up through the hole in the ceiling. He asked her to bring him some food and betel nut, and the new charged phone batteries. Wei agreed and came out at daybreak the next day. She searched for an hour, but then saw the branch stuck up from a hole in the ground. It was the right place. The wind was blowing fiercely so it was difficult to hear one another through the hole, but the cell phones worked fine. They didn't worry

Continuin' On

about the charge because she would return every other day with a new charge. She dropped the supplies down to Amos on a fishing line.

Amos asked what the family and fiends were saying. Wei said, in her broken Chinese, "Everyone misses you. They wish you were still alive."

Amos said, "How about the bill collectors? Are they bothering you?"

"They did for awhile. But they feel like everyone else, that the sharks got you. The ones that keep coming over were chased away by your older bother."

He asked, "Is my plan okay with you? Will you be okay?"

"I'm fine. I have our son and my jobs. Your father checked, and the government won't deport me."

Amos said that he would stay in the cave until the rosaries were finished. He had a friend with a twenty-six foot motorboat that would take him to Guam. He asked Wei to round up three hundred dollars to gas up the boat.

It was later related that the rosaries were serious events with a lot of praying, wailing, and remembrances. Everyone contributed food every night for the rosary, and Wei managed to skim off a share for Amos in the cave. The family also donated money for Wei, and she saved this money for the gas for the boat. Wei found Amos' passport and dropped it down into the cave with food and new batteries. Amos called his friend Gregorio with the boat.

After twenty-five days in the cave, Amos swam out through the hole in the wall to the ocean at low tide. His friend, Gregorio picked him up outside the cave and off they went on the perilous, open ocean ride to Guam. They made it safely, fighting some eight foot rollers along the way. They entered the Guam

Harbor in broad daylight, ready for immigration and customs. They were legal, and Amos' escape to Guam went off without a snag. Amos swore Gregorio to secrecy about the trip, and his friend's reply was simply, "Not to worry, Brah. I hate those fucking bill collectors."

Several of the family members came to us at the investigations agency, and asked us to review all the police and rescue reports, and to make background and computer checks. Of course, Amos' name came up unfavorably in financial and credit reports. But he didn't have a criminal record, or was wanted for anything in the world, or had not re-established himself elsewhere, unless with another name. INTERPOL had never heard of him.

Three weeks later, a family member said that he had been told from a friend that Amos had been spotted in Guam or a definite look-alike. The friend also knew Gregorio, and when he told Gregorio said he had seen Amos in Guam, Gregorio just looked away and didn't say anything. Amos' father, Hidalgo, came in with a five hundred dollars retainer and two plane tickets, and asked that Carlos and I check out the Guam sighting.

One hour later, we were in Guam with Amos' photos and his pertinent identification. Through a contact at Motor Vehicles, Carlos found out that Amos had a new driver license with his current address. He lived in Yigo where construction was going hot and heavy. Amos had no special skills but was considered a competent handyman on a job site. We checked his home address, a large rundown apartment complex. No one was home, but a neighbor said he usually got home at six PM, and confirmed he was working construction. In 2008, a large contingent of US Marines was moving from Okinawa, and Guam was getting ready for the new influx of military growth. There were lots

Continuin' On

of jobs, and the value of property was going sky-high.

Amos came home on time. We knew it was him by the photographs, and he was chewing betel nut. We walked over and introduced ourselves.

He responded by saying, "I don't have anything to say to you guys. Just leave."

I said, "Amos, that won't work. Your father hired us to find you, and to convince you to come back."

"I'm not going back. I like it here just fine. The family wouldn't understand."

A beautiful *Chamorita* walked over to us. She said, "What's going on? I'm Maria Gonzales. I'm his girl friend."

Carlos answered, "We're from a private investigation agency, and Amos' father wants him to come home to Saipan."

She looked at Carlos and said, "Why talk to Henry? He's from Rota."

I nodded at Amos and said, "Here's your step on the way back to honesty."

Amos said, "He's right. My name is Amos and I'm from Saipan."

Maria grimaced and said, "Did you tell me anything that's true? Do you love me? Oh shit, you're probably married."

I nodded at him again and said, "You're on a roll. You might as well be honest."

He said, "Yeah, I love you. But I'm married and have a son."

She said, "How can you do this to me. You said we had a future together. I want to slap you!"

"I really do love you. Don't give up on me, okay? I'm going to straighten up everything on Saipan. My father will help me. I married a Chinese girl as a convenience thing for her and me."

Amos told us that he was working steady, and had been paying his bills. He and Maria excused themselves. They seemed to be getting it together in their quiet talk over under a giant mango tree. No slapping or yelling. That was a good sign.

Amos came over and said, "Here's the deal. Maria said that she would stick with me for now. I'll come over to Saipan on my days off, Saturday and Sunday, and talk to my family." It appeared the lad was finally growing up.

I said, "Sounds good. Let's get your father on the phone and make a commitment."

He said, "Damn, you have no mercy. This won't be easy."

Carlos said, "Look you've been gone for over two months. Your family is still worried. They want you back. You'll just have to work this situation with Wei and Maria. You can catch up on your bills with your new job."

He said, "Yeah, you're right. Please call my father."

I called Hidalgo and explained the whole situation. He was elated. Amos and he talked for twenty minutes. Amos agreed to spend Saturday and Sunday with his family. He wouldn't take Maria this time. She understood. But she was real clear that she didn't expect him to have a woman on each island.

Amos kept his word. The family had a welcome home party, kind of like for a person rising from the dead. He explained everything to Wei, and she was okay with their arrangement, as long as she didn't get deported or lose her son. Now he would have to maintain his new maturity and keep his job, pay the bills, and work out the future with Maria.

Someone in the family leaked the story to the media. Amos became "the one-day celebrity" in the newspapers, and the readers were amazed that a person could survive so long in a cave

Continuin' On

without food and water. No one mentioned Guam. Wisely, he declined all television interviews, claiming he would need several months to recover from the trauma and malnutrition. Wei, Maria, Hidalgo, Gregorio and everyone at the investigations agency maintained their silence.

10

LEO GOES SWIMMING

Any hotel owner or manager will tell you that a hotel is just a microcosm of everyday society. It's just a miniature world. Everyone eventually wants to go on vacation or on hiatus or just hide out for awhile. Some guests are good folks and some are assholes. Some tourists will never be happy at the beach or in a steak house, because they take their miserable selves with them on holiday. The Beach Hotel tried to accommodate them all. We could easily be rated as four-star plus hotel. The sandy beach is beyond words in beauty. Our amenities and activities are all eco-friendly. Up the road about a kilometer is a five-star hotel called the Island Retreat. It is a spectacular hotel, very expensive, and boasts of gold-plated bathtubs.

In between the two hotels are dozens of lots owned by local residents, with about a third of the lots being public land. Therefore the beach is always accessible to the island residents. This has a lot of advantages and some disadvantages. If you're a local person, you can get to the beach and have fun, rightfully

Continuin' On

so. The disadvantages for the hotels are that the repetitive thieves and trouble-makers can get past security by accessing from the beach. They also litter the beach with trash and betel nut spit. Some of the unlicensed vendors also harass the hotel guests as they are sun-bathing on the beach. Some are trying to sell drugs.

Local folks also build ugly tin huts along the beach, and have little farms. The little abodes are eyesores, but it could be argued that the beach has belonged to them for hundreds of years. Sometimes the youngsters party late and set off fireworks. There are no zoning or disturbance laws so anything goes. Grazing of farm animals is also allowed, and of course, on a hot day with no breeze, there's no doubt that cows and horse are fertilizing the land. The flies know it too, and they swoop down in droves.

Occasionally, however, the animals provide great entertainment for our guests. Most of our Japanese and Korean guests are city-dwellers, and have never owned or touched a cat or dog, or only ever seen horses and cows on television. Usually our local farmers and ranchers are friendly to the guests, and they let the children touch the animals, and they teach them how to feed the big critters. Horses became so popular, that I contracted with a local Japanese-Filipino man to buy some gentle horses and to take our guests on rides along the beach at low tide.

Pedro Pedrozo moved his giant bull Leo from the interior, down to his brother's property at the beach for some fresh air and a well-deserved rest. He built a temporary fence, with the posts mounted only in sand and clay. Leo has been on his mating rounds for three weeks at other ranches. Leo had a great reputation of having a healthy libido and his mating partners had about a sixty per cent conception rate. Twenty-six new calves owed their impressive genetics to Leo. Pedro has built a sizable bank account for his old age, thanks to Leo's fees. The bull was always ready to do his duty, but of late, he had been losing weight and needed a break. Pedro wasn't worried about the flimsy fence. He had never busted out in the past.

Leo was not only virile and strong, but he was bovine intelligent. He watched the horses leaving every day on the beach rides. In his little pea brain, or his instincts to be free, he decided to shove the temporary fence aside and follow the horses along the beach. With his 1500 pounds of pure Hereford stock, it was a simple manner of pushing the fence with his giant head and it collapsed. Making Leo safe to handle, Pedro had sawed off most of his horns. Goring wouldn't be a problem for those on the beach. Getting stomped on a by a mammoth animal could be a serious medical issue.

Pedro's friend, Rolando Guzman, tried to chase the animal back to Pedro's property. Leo was not about to be corralled. Rolando telephoned Pedro with a neighbor's cell phone. Pedro was quickly on the way from Marpi at the north end of the island.

Leo didn't know quite what to make of the ocean. He tried slurping the water. Obviously he didn't like the salt and minerals, and gave up drinking. He trotted after the horses. The sunbathers all ran from the beach, up into the jungle when they saw him.

As Leo neared the front of my hotel, several of the local boys on foot were trying to chase him back to Pedro's property. It would have been good to have Hawaiian *paniolos* on horseback.

It was obvious that Leo was enjoying his freedom too much, and he wasn't much worried about boys yelling and trying to make him turn around. Instead of going back up the beach, he ran directly into the Beach Hotel's garden and pool area. The yelling from the guests attracted Cocina's attention, and after

Continuin' On

seeing the big bull charging through her orchids, called me in my office. Carlos and I were finishing up reports on documents that we had served for local attorneys.

I said to Carlos, "You won't believe this."

"What have we got?"

"Carlos, we've another animal case, giant bull, right here in the hotel. By the pool."

"Yeah hoo! *Vamonos, vaqueros.* Where's my lasso?"

By the time we got there, Leo had panicked and fell in the swimming pool. He was thrashing and bellowing, splashing water in every direction and going from the shallow end to the deep end, not able to get out. As it turned out, he was a natural swimmer. He was totally frightened, and was leaving plenty of brown and yellow souvenirs in our formerly clear, crystal pool. The guests had retreated to the high floors and were looking down at Leo, and of course, at us, trying to figure out what we were going to do. Everyone had an opinion.

A local boy told us that Pedro was on the way. Cocina called the Fire Department. I asked Carlos to call Alfredo at the zoo. I had heard that he had a tranquilizer gun. Our maintenance foreman, Mario II, showed up and grinning, and said, "I better post a "no swimming" sign."

I said, "Mario, you laugh, but you're going to have a lot tile work to do. Have to change the water too. All that pooh-pooh."

Carlos took the humor a bit farther. He said, "If I go get my rifle, we can have a Guangman fix us up a deluxe barbeque tonight, all you can eat."

I got caught up in it. "The kids will love it. Leo-burgers on special. With every hamburger, you get a free whoopee cushion."

After swimming several laps of the pool, Leo tired out and

just stood in the shallow end. His eyes were bulging and rimmed in red, and it was hard to tell if he was completely pissed off or just confused, and probably ready for Pedro to lead him away. Getting caught in a swimming pool had not been his idea of freedom. He still let out an occasional snort, and kept shitting away. Every time he released another patty, I could hear the children letting out exclamations in several foreign languages that probably translated to, "Gross! Yuck!" The psychologists call it the transference of disgust. People get caught up in it, and it was going to be tough to get guests back into the pool, even when it was completely sanitized.

Pedro showed up with ropes and bags of carrots and candy. Leo saw Pedro, and shook his head from side to side. If bulls could smile, he'd be grinning from ear to ear. He stopped snorting and just stood still.

Pedro asked, "Do you think the tile stairs at the shallow end will hold him? I think I can lead him out. He's worn out and just wants some hay and grain."

I said, "Yeah, it'll hold him. Mario just finished rebuilding and remodeling the stairs."

Alfredo appeared with his tranquilizer gun. He said that he had a dart that wouldn't knock him out, just gentle him. Pedro said to hold off, and that he'd try to tempt him out with the taste treats.

Pedro walked in the pool and gently placed a lariat over Leo's head. He showed him the carrots and tried coaxing him out of the water to the stairway. He munched a few. Leo took two steps and then stopped. Pedro showed him the candy, and he started moving again. Each candy got about five steps out of Leo. The bull was in the mood for something sweet. He needed some sugar

Continuin' On

for energy. He walked up the stairs with Pedro. Once he reached the top onto level ground, he let out a giant fart, and then released two humongous patties next to Cocina's orchids. The kids on the balconies watching the rescue went wacko. This was better than any cartoon or inane movie that they had ever seen.

Leo walked happily and briskly alongside Pedro as they headed back to his corral. He had had his adventure and was ready for the fresh hay, and a long nap. He needed to rest up, and be prepared for his next romantic interlude. Making baby calves was obviously more fun that drinking salt water and falling in swimming pools.

Pedro came to the hotel that night to work out the damages. He said, "I got Leo back to his old corral in the mountains. He won't bother you and your guests any more."

Still into more humor, I responded, "Pedro, SHIT happens! The entertainment value to our guests should offset some of the expenses." He laughed.

I showed him the expense sheet. He could see it was a fair estimation for replacement of the water, cleaning and sanitizing every where, and repairing about 100 tiles. I said, "If that damn bull had eaten or smashed Cocina's orchids, a minor war could have developed."

Pedro said, "I know about ladies and their flowers. My wife is already arranging some new orchids from Johore, Malaysia for Cocina. She grows a lot of pink and white Slipper orchids, and a few light green and pink Hourais. She'll bring them over tomorrow."

I said, "Here's the deal. We're neighbors. Also, my friend Juan Del Nero has two heifers that need a visit from Leo. Do that and I'll cut the bill by fifty percent. Good for you?"

Pedro said, "I like it. *Si yu'us ma'ase*. I'll drop the check off tomorrow when we bring the orchids."

As the Frenchies like to say, *Une bonne blaque, bein?* Good joke, fun story eh?

II

OFF TO THE PHILIPPINES

Cocina organized a trip to San Pedro, Laguna Province to see all of her family and to celebrate our wedding, Filipino style. We had married a year ago at the Beach Hotel as part of a group wedding organized by the Matchmakers, George and Jo, with eleven other couples. Our children, Annie, Donna and Anthony were all anxious to see their *Pinoy* cousins. They went shopping in just about every store on Saipan and Guam, and managed to fill four large suitcases and five cardboard boxes with presents and souvenirs. We were loaded up with toothpaste, combs and brushes, q-tips, shampoo, lice rinse, soap, candy, and items hard to find in the Filipino countryside.

Our arrival in the Philippines was a memorable event at the airport. I met bunches of immediate relatives, and dozens more two and three times removed in the extended family. Getting to our hotel was no mean trick. It was Saturday evening, and all of Manila decided to go out at night to escape the daytime humid heat. The traffic was horrendous, but the hotel cozy and comfortable. By midnight, it was like Mandrake the Magician swung his magic baton, and like poof, all the greeters were gone, and only our nuclear family was left. A major wedding reception was planned for the next day in San Pedro. It would take three houses and several barbeques to accommodate the well-wishers.

The wedding party was planned by Cocina's mother Raphaela, and Cocina's sisters. The men did the barbeque, and afterwards the music. The ladies laid out the table and food presentation, special dishes like *Lechon Baboy* (roasted pig), *Adobong Manok* (chicken adobo), *Pansit Bihon* (white noodles), *Kalderetang Baka* (beef stew) and *Pritong Manok* (fried chicken), served with hot, local peppers. Very tasty and nutritious. The family kept bringing me food, and I would have to say *basug*.

I wore a long white *barong Tagalog* outside my shorts, and Cocina looked regal and heavenly in her pink traditional *terno* dress with the large butterfly sleeves. We were adorned in flower leis and mwar-mwars and anointed with native perfumes. Digital cameras were working overtime.

It was a foreign country to me, but so pleasant and relaxing. Everyone spoke English of varying degrees of proficiency and accents. There were lots of handshakes and backslaps, and it was a celebration of marriage and love, and meeting the *Americano* from Saipan. After several cases of San Miguel beer and local gin, some of the partying men had a few angry words with one another. But others pulled the men apart, gave them a few more beers, and the pushing and shoving were reduced to mere feeble attempts at being macho. No one pulled out any machetes.

Two days later, Cocina and I were off to Cebu and Mactan Island for our Filipino honeymoon. We flew in over the crystal clear lagoon. Bohol Strait separates Cebu and Mactan, and

Continuin' On

both islands have functional harbors and modern tourist facilities. History was made here on April 27, 1521. Mactan Island was the scene of a gory battle where the war party led by Chief Lapu-Lapu killed Portuguese explorer Ferdinand Magellan and sixty of his Spanish crew, using only bolos and *kris* (curved knives) against armor and firearms. The Spanish sailed for God, Glory and Gold into these territories, and the locals took umbrage with the Spanish ambitions.

Legend has it that the local warriors were upset about the foreigners invading their land and the sailors screwing their women. There wasn't much discussion, just a lot of slashing and cutting. Whatever the truth might be, the slaughter made Chief Lapu-Lapu a national hero, and no Spaniards stepped foot on Cebu or Mactan for another fifty years. Eventually the local tribes were overpowered and Cebu became the Spanish capital. Throughout the next centuries, the Spaniards intermingled with the local ladies, and the name *Cebuan* was given to the beautiful women from this region of the Philippines. Many of the Filipina actresses, television hostesses, and beauty queens hail from Cebu.

We timed our visit for the Black Nazarene Fiesta, and Cebu was loaded with tourists and people from the villages. The *kriminals* from Mindanao also knew about the celebration, and were there to do their nasty business. The hotel staff warned us to be careful, and not go out at night and walk the streets, as we were obvious targets. Next day, Cocina had her gold necklace torn off at a public market by a very fast teenager. She didn't chase him for fear that he had a knife. The woman had good sense. Her neck was bruised where he snapped off the necklace. Other than losing a favorite gift from her mother, she was fine, just a little nervous and upset. We looked around at the other shoppers and noticed that no one was wearing watches or jewelry except for shell necklaces and bracelets. Should have been a clue for us while visiting the public areas during festival times.

On the way back to the hotel in a taxi, we experienced a first hand account of a shoot-out like our own Wild West. Moments before we reached a main intersection, three armed gangsters jumped onto a jeepney, and took everything of value from the twelve passengers and driver. One of the men ordered the three school girls to raise their skirts and he fondled their *bebe's*. A sharp-eyed witness saw a police car fifty meters away and told the five police officers inside the car. Sometimes, if you're a kriminal, you have to consider an element of luck, good or bad, in your crimes. The kriminals expected a fast, simple robbery, and running off into the huge crowds.

It was not their day. The five officers were returning from firearms training and were fully equipped with semi-auto pistols and shotguns. When the robbers left the jeepney, they were greeted with five alert policemen, all of them trained, overflowing with adrenaline and their weapons loaded. One of the young robbers decided to raise his gun towards the officers. Within seconds and as we came around the corner in our taxi, three robbers lay dead. Some of the witnesses later claimed that the officers shot the men after they were down, execution-style. We didn't see anything like that, only the officers handcuffing the robbers after the gunfire, making sure that they didn't cause any more harm to anyone. A large male robbery victim walked over and spit on the corpse of the robber that had ordered the girls to raise their skirts. He yelled out, "Go to hell, *pendejo*." One of the violated girls was the man's daughter.

The following day, the local newspaper carried the story of

Continuin' On

twenty demonstrators at City Hall, complaining about over-reaction by the police. Three jeepney victims were interviewed on television, all commending the police, and thanking *Cristo* and the heavens for saving them from being shot. The mayor said that the case was investigated by the police chief within several hours, and that the shootings were justified. He asserted that there would no further action by the government, except for the return of the bodies to Mindanao. All three robbers had extensive criminal records involving violence, and one was suspected of a terror attack against the Philippines Army.

The remainder of the week was filled with love and romance, and plenty of fresh fruit and tasty combinations of fruits and vegetables, and *halo-halo*. I bought Cocina another gold necklace just like the gift from her mother Raphaela, so her mother wouldn't have to know and worry about the theft at the public market. Her neck healed quickly. All those days of honeymoon splendor eventually end, and off we went back to the realities of San Pedro, and our three kiddies, and the rest of the family. Of course, anything or anyone are good reasons for a fiesta in the Philippines, so we had a welcome-home party. We only needed two houses for this celebration. Some of the family members had to tend to their farms, and couldn't get away.

12

THE PROLIFIC MAYOR

On our return to San Pedro, the big news involved the murder of Rey Espina, the mayor of the nearby town of Santa Barbara. According to the television news, Rey had been shot off his motorcycle by his son, Rodolfo, while he was riding through town looking at some city construction projects.

Rey Espina was a legend throughout the Laguna Province. Even in his sixties, he was handsome and fit, with a long handlebar mustache. He was a flamboyant, colorful character, who always wore a white cowboy hat. He was quite impressive riding his chopper Harley, and being a local version of a benevolent Mafia godfather. He had a loyal following, and was the one who decided if someone would get a job, or be forgiven for some transgression. He appointed the members of the Electoral Commission, and also decided who would work at the polls. Surprisingly, he never lost an election.

But Rey needn't have worried about winning an election. He fathered over eighty children, who were mostly adults now

Continuin' On

and on the town payroll. Combined with the offspring's in-laws, there were plenty of reliable votes. Many of the women in town claimed to be his past lovers, and their children part of his lineage. Rey didn't acknowledge them all, and as with the Kings and Queens of Europe, there was infighting and confusion about who would take over control when Rey retired or crossed over to the other side. The young boys talked about who would get the chopper, or the cowboy hat.

Rey had one obvious weakness, which upset many of the town's people. He liked to break in young teenage virgins, some as young as fifteen. Conversely, other parents encouraged their daughters to go with Rey, because maybe, just maybe, the parents would end up with a job. The young girls invigorated him, and made him feel young again. He never used a condom, so many of the girls became pregnant, and thus, his reputation for the many offspring. With some of the girls, he took responsibility. Others he just said that the girls slept around and the baby likely belonged to someone else. DNA testing didn't exist in the province.

He had been watching a young girl named Evangeline Codilla grow up. She was now fifteen, and a real head-turner. She was *maganda* and model material, and was smart beyond her years. She already knew of her feminine wiles, and how to flirt, and get her way with males. When Rey asked her over for a cold drink, she jumped on his motorcycle, and off they went to his hill-top home. She was still a virgin, but she knew what Rey wanted. She was ready for him, and for the thrill of sex, but her mind was buzzing for the right trade-off. She wanted gold, but she also wanted a college education. She would have him pay for the college, or make a call to the dean for zero tuition fees.

Rey would have promised her the *Macapagal Palace* at this

stage. But he agreed to the gold necklace and to two years of college tuition. She gave him what he wanted, and to her delight, she too enjoyed the arrangement. He was a sensitive, caring lover, and because she had practiced over several years of masturbation, they were both totally and physically satisfied within minutes. She didn't worry about being pregnant, because her girl friends knew where to get the "morning-after pill."

Evangeline hadn't told her mother about riding off with Rey.

Rudolfo was one of Rey's sons. He was twenty years old, no skills or education, but expected to have a good-paying job because of his father. The Philippines has over eighty million people, with few jobs at low pay, and millions of those people living in poverty and barely make a day-to-day living. Rey considered Rudolfo to be immature and somewhat dull, and had not found him a job. Rudolfo was angry and embarrassed.

Rudolfo also had his eye on Evangeline and really needed a job so that he could propose marriage. When he heard that the girl had ridden off with his father, he knew that his chances of winning her over, and appreciating her virginity, were gone. He went to his home to find his revolver.

Rey delivered Evangeline back home on his motorcycle. As he stopped in front of her home, Serena Beram came out of the house. Rey knew her right away as one of his past lovers. Evangeline could see that Serena was angry, but figured it was just because she had ridden off with the mayor. But she soon learned differently.

Serena yelled, "What are you doing with the girl?"

Witnesses later related that the Rey could hardly answer, except to say, "We just took a ride on the chopper."

"You stupid, foolish man. Evangeline is your daughter from

Continuin' On

our dating days."

Rey answered, "I had no idea. You never told me."

"I was so embarrassed, I moved away for awhile. You fucked her, didn't you? You fucked your own daughter."

Evangeline put her head down, and started crying. She said, "Mama, you never told me who my father was."

Rey was dumfounded, said that he was sorry, and got on his motorcycle to leave.

Rodolfo arrived on his bicycle, pulling out his revolver. He had heard most of the conversation. He pointed the gun at his father, Rodolfo said, "You had to take her away from me. Then I find out we both had you as our father. You piece of shit."

Rey weakly said, "Son, I didn't know. I'm sorry."

"You deserve to die. Fucking your own daughter." Rudolfo fired at close range, three rounds hitting Rey fully in the chest. He fell off his motorcycle, dead before he hit the dirt. Rudolfo threw down his revolver, sat down, and waited for the authorities. Serena and Evangeline ran in the house sobbing, and holding each other.

As these tragedies go, the police arrived and took Rudolfo into custody. He would have to ask for a change of venue in the court hearing, as all the local judges were appointed by his father. There would be no fairness for him in Santa Barbara. Evangeline got her morning-after pill, and she and her mother moved to live with an aunt some seventy kilometers up north. She vowed to be more careful about her next lover. Several hundred town workers were nervous about their jobs and the upcoming special election.

Greek philosopher Nikos Kazantzakis wrote, "We come from the dark abyss, we return to the dark abyss, and we call the luminous interval "life." And Rey Espina certainly had a full and bright life. He would be remembered in legend and family trees, good or bad, for his small part of eternity.

The murder made for good *tsismis* in San Pedro for several days. The gossip was eclipsed when we got a call from Saipan that Cocina's sister, Dina Miradora, had been missing for three days under questionable circumstances. Time to go home. I called Carlos and asked him to get the reports from the Commissioner. Carlos had heard that it was a dead-end case, that Dina was just hiding with someone, and that she was having immigration problems. Her clothes and make-up were still at her house. The police figured that she would be back home after a few days.

13

DINA IS MISSING ON SAIPAN

We left Manila and were back on Saipan in ten hours. We timed the flight perfectly. Carlos met us at the airport with the sketchy details that were available. Cocina had six siblings, and Dina was the baby in the family. She was only twenty-six years old, never married or had children, and had been going steady with a local guy. This was the fourth day of her disappearance.

Carlos said the local cops had done very little in the investigation. He said, "They wrote the whole thing off as a girl who ran away with her boyfriend, Nick Companos. But when I checked with the Tinian ferry and the airport, there was no record of her leaving the island. I checked Nick on his job at the market, and found him working in the warehouse. He didn't seem worried or concerned, and hadn't joined in on the search for Dina."

I said, "This is weird, like she just disappeared into thin air, and no one seems to care. Did the cops run a poster with a photo on television or the newspapers?"

Carlos answered, "No posters or television and radio announcements. But her friends and I have got all the bases covered. Tomorrow her photo will be in all the papers, including Guam and the internet news. I'll be interviewed for television and radio tomorrow. We're doing a press conference at the hotel."

Cocina said, "Did anyone check with the neighbors? Nick has been physically abusive to her before. She tried to break up with him, but he refused to break up and kept coming back. There should be a restraining order on that guy in the court or at the police station. Dina had her own copy, pinned to the kitchen wall."

I said, "It's late. We'll tackle this situation in the morning. Right now, we have to get home to the children and make sure that they're okay and not too worried."

The children were fine. We woke up at daybreak, and I paged the commissioner, Lois Harding. I knew she would be awake. This was her work-out day at the gym. She answered within minutes. I invited her down to the hotel for breakfast. She was on her second circuit of weights and machines, and said that she'd see us in about forty-five minutes.

She joined us right on schedule. Carlos and I were already having our Starbuck Kenya coffee. Guangman said to forget the menu, that he had a special Asian breakfast cooking for us. He also brought us the newspapers with the "Missing Person – Information Request" posters that showed Dina's happy, smiling face.

I asked, "Anything new on Dina?" I showed the commissioner the photos.

She said, "Nothing. The investigators told me that it was simply a case of the girl running away with her boyfriend, probably to either Rota or Guam."

Continuin' On

When I told her what Carlos had discovered in a few hours, she said, "Those numb nuts. I asked them if they had done all the routine things, they said that they had."

I asked, "You know about the domestic violence cases and the restraining order?"

She said, "They told me about that. They said that the missing girl and the boyfriend had gotten back together."

Cocina joined us and said, "That's bullshit. She tried over and over to get rid of that guy, and he wouldn't go away."

Lois looked at Carlos, "You haven't turned in your badge yet, so work this case some more. I'll get you some backup from Fred and Alfonso. You know them, right?"

Carlos said, "Yeah, they're good guys. But right now, Tom and I can handle this end. Maybe your guys could check with all the neighbors, and maybe talk to Nick and find out what he knows. Then Tom and will talk to him a second time later in the week."

After the promise of help and cooperation, the commissioner left. I looked at Carlos and said, "What's with those stupid motherfuckers? They couldn't find their assholes with their own hands."

Carlos grinned, and said, "Tom, relax. We've been through this before. Most of the cops are GED's and are politically connected. Most of them couldn't pass any kind of entrance or physical fitness exam. You now that, so why get excited? You are in the islands, my friend. Watch your blood pressure."

Cocina said, "I know why it's bothering him, and me. Everybody loves Dina, so why in the hell aren't they working her case?"

Carlos replied, "You've got to brace yourself for some bad news. We'll hope for the best, but when someone is gone almost a week, there's usually a serious reason to be missing this long."

I said, "Assholes, they should have worked it from Day 1. Let's go to work, Carlos. *Arribe,* Amigo."

He said, "I'll do the press conference in an hour, and off to work."

I said, "Let's shake some bushes, and turn over some rocks. Let's see what crawls out. Maybe some cockroaches!"

"Please find Dina. She's my baby sister." Cocina left for her office, head bowed, trying to hide her tears.

14

FINDING DINA

The press conference was productive. The newswoman did an excellent interview, and the photographer took a series of photos of Dina that Cocina was able to find in her scrapbook. The media seemed sincerely concerned about Dina. Now, the publicity part and an appeal to the public for information were in full swing. The Filipino community managed to raise two thousand dollars for information leading to an arrest of the suspect. Cocina contributed another three thousand dollars. Money talks and five thousand dollars is a definite incentive to break loose with information.

Cocina went with us to Dina's apartment, a small one bedroom on a street several blocks from the coast. The yellow police investigation tape had been torn down, and the front door lock busted. The apartment had been thoroughly ransacked. Cocina started crying, "How can people do this? They took all her clothes and make-up, and even her panties and bras. The *kriminals* cleaned out the kitchen and took everything in the refrigerator. How can people be so mean?"

Carlos and I just nodded. We both knew how cruel people can be to one another. The average person doesn't know, or wants to ignore, that there are people that will kill you for a pair of shoes, or kill you for the sheer enjoyment of watching you take your last breath. Some killers even talk about the gurgling sound of a cut throat, as the victim dies and the eyes beg for mercy. After talking to these sleazy killers, your first inclination is to squash them like a poisonous bug, but then your humanity kicks in, and you have to settle for a long tequila shot and a shower.

The court restraining order had been removed from its place on the wall. Someone thought it important enough to take away.

It was unlikely that we would find fingerprints of the killer. Everything had been touched and moved around. If the killer was Nick, his fingerprints would be present anyway. But just for the case file, we lifted about eighteen prints for later investigation. There was little chance of finding any other workable physical evidence. We used our investigation kit, and found no blood or semen stains. Carlos took over one hundred photographs with his new digital camera.

Cocina observed nothing of importance. There were no notes and letters, and no diary in Dina's personal bills and receipts. All of her paperwork was scattered around the bedroom. Her passport and immigration cards were missing.

As we were packing up our gear, a neighbor came over, and said, "I know who did all the stealing."

I said, "Yeah, who?"

The neighbor answered, "Is the reward still good? My information could lead to the killer."

"The reward is there for the right information, and not some made-up story. And maybe it was just thieves that took all of

Continuin' On

Dina's stuff."

He said, "A lot of people went through the house. Some of them were her friends. But I also saw Nick, the boyfriend, going through everything. I looked through a side window. He carried out a duffel bag that was bulging, like it was really full."

I asked, "When was Nick here?"

He said, "Yesterday, right after the police left. He knocked down the police tape and came out with that loaded duffel bag. He was in there for about ten minutes."

I asked, "Did you call the police?"

"Yep, I called them, but they didn't get out here for over two hours. Probably having donuts and a chew afterwards."

The neighbor gave us a preliminary list of the people that had gone in the house after Nick had left. Most of them he knew by nicknames. Cocina knew them all, and was disgusted. She asked, "Why didn't they call me? If they wanted something to remember her by, I would have given it to them. That's the Filipino way of sharing."

I said, "Too late to fret now. Let's keep working." We dropped Cocina off at the hotel and met with the commissioner at Java Joe's Coffee Shop. We gave her the list of people that had been in the house, and let her know about Nick. She said that her investigators would talk to everyone on the list, and then Nick. She had run a complete check on Nick and found out that besides his domestic violence arrest on Saipan, he also had six arrests on Guam for felonies, one of which was a homicide. The homicide file found him to be viable person of interest, but couldn't take him to court. The evidence was too thin, and the eyeball witness was not credible.

Later in the week, we spoke to the police investigators. They had all the full names of the people that had ransacked the house, and wanted to know if Cocina wanted to press charges. The interview with Nick was non-productive. He appeared to hardly even know his own name. He played dumb the whole time.

Nick admitted being Dina's boyfriend, but he said, once she got the retraining order, he knew it was over and quit visiting or calling her. He admitted being at the house and taking away a duffel bag of odds and ends. He said that the police tape had already been torn down when he arrived at Dina's house. When he entered the house, someone ran out the back door. He didn't know this person and couldn't provide a description because it happened so fast. He said that he took only his own clothes, and a walkman and portable CD player. He denied taking her passport or any official documents.

The investigators described Nick as one cool character, and knew by his responses that he had been interviewed many times before by cops. He declined to take a polygraph examination. He told the investigators, "My lawyers always tell me, never, never take a lie detector test. They're just too unreliable."

I called Cocina on the cell phone and asked if she wanted to press charges on the looters at Dina's house. I read her the final list of names. Again, she was shocked. Some of the people had been good family friends. She had helped several of them find jobs on Saipan. She wanted a gold watch, gold earrings, and a gold bracelet, back from the looters. She added that the watch and jewelry had sentimental value, and if she got them back, there would no follow-up on the case. The investigators told five of the interviewees about the deal and the items all came back within to the hotel within three days. There would be no prosecution for theft.

Continuin' On

It was time for Carlos and me to talk to Nick. We had no workable information, nothing to go on, and he probably knew that. He came to the hotel voluntarily, and we found a quiet room to talk. The investigators were right. He was relaxed, and answered all our questions with precise concentration. He admitted to his past criminal record, and also that he and Dina had some arguments, but never approaching violence.

Carlos asked him in blank, "Do you know what happened to Dina?"

He said, "I have no idea. One day she was there and the next day she was gone."

I asked, "Did you kill her?"

Nick said, "No, I didn't, and before you ask your next question, I'll tell you outright. I don't know anything about her disappearance or death, or anyone that might have killed her. I didn't hire anyone to do it."

Carlos asked, "Did you kick in the door?"

"No, the lock was busted when I got there. I still have my key anyway."

I asked, "Did you take the retraining order off the wall?"

"Yeah, I took it. It's our business, no one else."

I said, "You don't seem too broken up about her disappearance."

He gave me his most sincere look, and said, "I told you, we were through. There was no emotion then, or now. She was a good screw. She had great lips. Do I wish her dead? No, I don't. She was a nice person, and deserved to have a long happy life, just not with me. That's all I know." He got up to leave, and didn't offer to shake hands.

We watched Nick through the window. He didn't seem in

hurry or the least bit troubled. He was either a psychopath without feelings, or he was innocent, at least in relation to killing Dina.

The commissioner and her crew threw Dina's disappearance in the cold case file. There was nothing new, and there was no sign of her in any of the computer files in the Philippines, Guam or Saipan. The investigators moved on to new cases. There are always plenty of those at any police department.

Carlos and I re-interviewed everyone and nothing developed. We increased the reward for information to ten thousand dollars, and still no tips. It hurt me to tell Cocina that Dina's case was on hold. There was nothing to do, but wait for developments.

We closed out Dina's apartment, her bills and accounts, told her employer, and gave the immigration authorities an update. Cocina handled these chores like a strong, capable sister. Sometimes she would pull over to the side of the road, and start trembling. It was all part of the grieving process. She didn't want a memorial service until we had some definite facts.

15

WHITEY ESCAPES FROM THE ZOO

One of the most popular attractions on Saipan is the Magic Castle Show at the Two Towers Hotel. Besides the magician "right from Las Vegas" Alfredo, the star of the show is Whitey, the white tiger. The magician lets everyone know that white tigers are not a separate species. They are the result of both parents having a recessive gene for white coloration. They re very rare in the jungle because their white color inhibits their ability to catch prey. Mostly they are bred in captivity. Whitey was usually a placid animal and was five years old. He was thoroughly trained for his act, and seemed content to live out his life in show business. Whitey wasn't a giant of his species but a good size—he was 515 pounds and nine feet long—but he was strong and intelligent.

On his non-working days or on the off hours, Whitey lodged in at the Saipan Zoo. He had a special cage built just for him, with lots of space and shade. He enjoyed a special meat diet, mainly frozen steaks and roasts from Oklahoma. He ate some local deer, when it was thrown in his cage. Even when comfortable, freedom is always in the mind of a cat. They like to roam. Fate stepped in one day as Whitey was having that exact urge. One of his keepers at the zoo, Jimbo Jimenez, had another and different urge. He was in a hurry to see his girl friend, and accidentally left the cage door partially closed. Whitey pushed at the gate with his oversize head. He was probably looking for another five pound roast. The gate swung open, and the jungle was only forty meters away.

Although it was sweltering outside the cage, Whitey decided that he could cross the hot grassy area, and be in the cool jungle in seconds. Off he went, and traveled higher up the mountains. Tigers can travel up to thirty-five miles per hour. Jimbo was around the corner from the cage, making out with his girl friend. He wasn't thinking about the cat. He was calculating if this was the day to unsnap his girl friend's bra.

Alfredo, the magician, usually retrieved his tiger several hours before the show, so he could calm him down and run him through several of his tricks. Of course, when he got to the tiger's cage, there was no Whitey. He went looking for Jimbo, and when he found the zoo keeper and the girlfriend, Jimbo was well past the bra stage, and was slipping off her jeans. He knocked on the rolled-up windows of the zoo truck.

Jimbo yelled out, "Hey, what is it?"

"It's me, dumb-ass. Where is my tiger?"

"Yeah, yeah. Give us a minute."

The girl friend jumped out the passenger side of the truck, trying to put on her panties and jeans. She ran off into the jungle, with hot sun reflecting off her white butt.

Jimbo got dressed. He said that he had fed Whitey, and locked the gate.

Continuin' On

Alfredo said, "The rules of the zoo are clear that you close the gate, and then put on the padlock. You didn't do that, and Whitey is gone. If he gets hurt, or he hurts someone, it'll be your ass. You're one dumb shit!"

The girl friend never did return. Jimbo ran alongside Alfredo, saying that he was sorry, and would help find Whitey. Alfredo reached inside his truck and found his tranquilizer gun and several leashes and ropes. They started up the hill, watching for Whitey's tracks. After several hours, they knew their search was pointless without some extra help. Whitey could easily be miles ahead up the mountains.

Alfredo called his boss at the hotel, and said that the show would have to be cancelled. He also called the police and spoke to the commissioner. He asked that once Whitey was cornered up or in a tree, to give him a call and he would go anywhere on the island. He was afraid that Whitey would panic and become dangerous, and then the police would have to shoot him.

Lois Harding activated the entire department. This was simply a situation of "protection and service" that had to be handled expeditiously. She was determined to get the cat before it could hurt anyone. She loved animals, and had seen the show with Whitey, but knew that his life was secondary to any human. She would save him if she could. She had her public information officer contact the television and radio stations, and the newspapers. To get Whitey fast, she would need everyone watching and to be aware of his or her personal safety.

Lois called us, and soon Carlos and I were on the move. Carlos knew the island, so we decided to head over to the back side of the zoo, maybe about four miles from where Whitey escaped. Jokingly I asked Carlos to find us some pith helmets and maybe summon some trekkers to set us up a jungle camp.

Carlos had apparently missed all the Tarzan movies, and gave an expression which probably translated to, "What the hell are you talking about?"

Whitey's first sighting was in San Roque. Whitey was seen running through some mango trees, with some boonie dogs right on his heels. One of the dogs bit him on the hind quarter, so he stopped and sunk his teeth in a few of the mutts, and they took off scurrying through the underbrush. Whitey scrambled over the mountain east of the Village of Tanapag. Lois organized a rough perimeter of the area, and moved her troops towards a center north of the mango trees. Alfredo joined her with his tranquilizer gun. She made an announcement over the police bands to avoid shooting the tiger if possible, and to avoid shooting each other in a crossfire. She brought up some customs dogs, hoping to tree the tiger, and let Alfredo do his job with the tranquilizer gun.

Whitey slipped through the circle of officers, and the next sighting was at the back of the Legislature. He was clever and a survivor. Whitey was running full blast, and was carrying something large and white in his mouth. He headed east down the mountain, to the back side of the Kingfisher Golf Course. Lois had requested a military helicopter for observation from Guam, but it hadn't arrived. Moments later, the chopper pilot reached Lois on the radio, and said that he was in sight of the golf course.

The pilot said, "Hey, I see the tiger. He's heading to the beach. Let your dogs go on both sides of the golf course, and maybe we get him onto to one of the limestone eroded mounds." The dogs did their job and surrounded him, and chased him to the top of

Continuin' On

the mound. Three of the SWAT officers were aiming their sniper rifles at him. Every time he tried to get down, one or two of the dogs would chase him back up. The shooters were tense and ready to fire, and were definitely not going to let him escape.

Whitey was still carrying the large white object in his mouth. Lois and Alfredo got there before any shots were fired. Alfredo yelled out a command to Whitey to stop. The tiger spotted Alfredo and heard his voice. He stopped snarling; apparently feeling now that he was safe from the dogs. The large white object fell from his mouth, and rolled down the mound. It was a human skull.

The dogs jumped all over the skull and were close to breaking it apart. One of the handlers got the dogs under control, and I gathered up the skull, and put it in my packsack. There was still some hair and dried flesh attached to the skull.

The dog handlers gathered up the dogs. Alfredo loaded his gun with a small-dose tranquilizer dart, and walked up the mound to Whitey. The tiger had stopped making any noise, and just lay down, watching Alfredo. Whitey made a sound very close to a housecat purring. He was happy to see Alfredo. As the tiger was distracted by a yelping dog, Alfredo fired his dart, hitting the tiger on the right haunch. He let out a horrendous roar.

I could swear Whitey was smiling within ten minutes as the dart took effect. Alfredo walked up to him, petted him several times and talked to him in a soft voice. Alfredo applied his collar and a heavy chain, and the two of them started walking up the trail to the zoo truck. Whitey stumbled along like he had been a bar all night, drinking tequila shooters.

I asked Alfredo how he knew what dosage to use on the dart. He said, "You figure the weight of the animal, and how passive you want him to be. I knew that I wanted him to be mellow and be able to walk. I couldn't imagine trying to carry him up the mountain to the truck. That little furry critter weighs over five hundred pounds."

Once Whitey was safely back in his zoo cage, Carlos and I drove over to the commissioner's office with the skull. There were plenty of flesh and hair to get DNA for identification, and the teeth were still intact. In my gut, I felt that we had just found Dina, or part of Dina. Where was the rest of the body?

16

SKULL TO THE CRIME LAB

The commissioner had the skull packaged properly and sent off to the crime lab on Guam for forensic examination. She requested that Dina's family respond to the hospital for DNA analyses to build up the biological profile. Cocina, several of her first cousins, and our children had samples drawn. Dina had no blood work on file. Her dental records were in the Philippines. Lois had her medical and dental files requested through official channels.

I noticed that the teeth in the skull were almost perfect with a few minor fillings. Cocina said was what Dina's teeth would be. The wisdom teeth were still intact. The hair on the skull was black, but that would be the case for most of the Filipinas. DNA—*deoxyribonucleic acid* identification would be available through the dried flesh, the bulb of the hair pieces, and the center root area of the teeth. We had to develop this physical evidence to match up with Dina or any other missing person.

Carlos and I met with the police investigators Fred and Alfonso, and Lois. Our job now was to backtrack on Whitey's trail through the jungle and over the mountains, and find where the skull had came from, and where the rest of the body might be. There are no predators on Saipan, like wolves and bears, but the boonie dogs might have messed up and scattered the rest of the bones. It had rained, so many of Whitey's tracks had been washed out. The customs and police dogs were given a shot, but came up with nothing. Rain also plays hell with scent.

A good friend, Chuck McNealy, had come out from Arizona to find a bride. He was staying at the hotel. He was a well-known hunter and tracker in the US, and was often written up for his work in well-publicized cases.

I found Chuck out by the pool, next to his new Chinese lady friend. I told him about the case, and he said that he was interested. He threw on his flip-flops and headed for his room to get his jungle khakis and hiking boots. Within twenty minutes, we were in my pick-up and heading for the spot where Whitey has been captured. Carlos said that he would join us after he picked up a topographical map from the Department of Interior.

Chuck said, "We'll start backtracking from here to the location where he was spotted with the skull, and then to where he was chased by the boonie dogs. It isn't logical to re-work his whole route from the zoo. So our best bet is that the body was between the Legislature and the mango trees. Or maybe the dogs moved the skull from the body from another location, or the killer cut up the body and left pieces all over the island."

I said, "Sounds like we've got a lot of jungle stomping coming up."

Chuck replied, "Yep, appears so. We'll be kicking up a lot of bugs and mosquitoes. I've got my long pants and long sleeve shirt on, and some mosquito repellant. I hate those squeeters."

Continuin' On

We found several tracks of the cat running from the ocean to the Legislature, and also some broken branches, where he ran helter-skelter through the brush. Once on top of the mountain, we worked out way westward down to the mango trees. We saw a few more tracks. Chuck knew where to look, and took his time, and marked some trees with his bowie knife, so we could avoid circling back over the same areas. Half-way down the mountain, we came across an old farm shed. It was deserted, but there was a rough road coming up from the area of the mango trees. There were banana trees planted everywhere. In back of the trees, were eight-foot, mature marijuana plants, about a thousand, with plenty of heavy buds. It was *cannabis sativa* in full bloom. The THC would be off the scale on those beauties. The plants would have been impossible to see from aerial surveillance, hiding under the mango trees and blending in with the bananas.

There were dozens of marijuana branches drying inside the shed. There were also scales and baggies. The leaves were dry enough to pack up.

Carlos made contact with us with his cell phone. We explained where we were, and he came up the dirt road from below in his Nissan Frontier 4-wheel drive. He found us at the farm shed, and told us that the road was almost impassable. No one had used the road in three-four days. We were glad to see Carlos. He was still on the police payroll and was carrying a 9mm Glock pistol. Marijuana farmers get very upset when you find and walk through their fields.

We used a grid pattern search for the body remains, walking sections in straight lines. Within minutes, Chuck let out a yell that he had found a shallow grave with a pile of bones, missing a skull. It had been dug up and the bones scattered, maybe when

Whitey was looking for food. There were several tiger prints around the grave.

Another shallow grave was only a few meters away. The ground was soft from the rain. I kicked away the dirt on the corner of the grave, and a set of feet was exposed. Carlos found two more. It appeared that we had come across a body dump area, surrounded and hidden by marijuana plants and banana trees, all under large, spreading mango trees. This little graveyard was going to clear up many of the missing person's reports.

I called the commissioner on her private line. I gave her the basic details, along with the road description and the Global Positioning System positioning. The GPS coordinates on the new cell phones are invaluable and usually pinpoint an area to within five meters. The twenty-four satellites circling the earth are always on duty.

I suggested that she call the FBI and request their forensics team. This was not the time for the local amateur detectives to screw up an investigation. We needed the experts. We also talked about setting up a surveillance crew to watch who might come to the farm. We would have to hide or vacate the farm. Meanwhile, Carlos was busily using his digital camera, documenting the area before the digging started.

Lois arrived about an hour later, along with her local, trusted investigators, Fred and Alfonso. She had sandwiches and coffee. It had been a long time since lunch. The FBI was fully cooperative and offered to help in any way possible. Since most of the victims were likely to be nationals from China and the Philippines, they would have international jurisdiction to assist with the case. A forensics team would come from Honolulu, probably within twenty-four hours. This crime scene and investigation would be

Continuin' On

a worldwide story.

Lois decided it would be good tactics to surveil the location until the FBI forensics team showed up. We figured the pot farmer would be up soon to package up his leaves to sell. It started to rain. Carlos hid his truck back in the jungle, and Lois left for the police station. The rain would cover up the truck tracks on the dirt road. Fred and Alfonso were both armed, and Lois had left her police shotgun with us. Chuck opted for the shotgun. He was not only a tracker and hunter, but also a gunsmith and range master.

It made me a little nervous when Chuck casually said, "Shit, I haven't killed anyone in several years." Carlos grimaced a bit, and then his face relaxed, as much to say, "Oh well, we'll just stay of the firing zone."

Being an experienced islander, Carlos built dry shelters for us, using the farmer's tools and machete. Lois promised to trek back through the jungle with more food and coffee, and some flashlights. At this stage, the fewer people knowing about the graves, the better.

As the sun was setting, we noticed a pair of headlights coming up the dirt road. Game time. It was a red Toyota Tacoma, just like the one used by Juan Riviera when he and his pals raped Mei Lee. The truck stopped in front of the shed, and shone its lights into the shed. Two men left the vehicle and walked to the shed. As they stepped in front of the headlights, Carlos yelled, "Stop! Police! Raise your arms straight over your head."

The man from the driver's door shouted back, "What the hell? Is this some kind of joke? You guys got your payoff." He didn't raise his arms, and started to turn around.

Carlos ordered, "Stop right there and raise your arms."

The man said, "Fuck off. Go get some donuts."

Chuck racked a round into his 12 gauge shotgun. It was a precise, identifiable sound like no other, especially in the quiet jungle at night. Both men stopped moving and raised their arms.

Carlos said, "Now we have your attention, lay down on your bellies with your arms out-stretched. If you go for your pockets, you're dead."

The man on the passenger side looked over towards the jungle on his right, his body tensing to run. Alfonso walked out of the shadows, and the man shrugged, and lay facedown down on the ground. Carlos ordered them to put their arms behind their back. They complied. Fred holstered his pistol, moved forward and handcuffed them. We quickly separated the two men for interrogation.

The driver said that his name was Leandro Cruz. He said that the farm belonged to the Riviera family, and that he was running an errand for Juan, just picking up some marijuana for the family and friends. He denied knowing about drug sales or about any graves. A tsunami of bullshit followed.

The passenger, Richardo Zambales, was nervous and stuttering. He said to Fred, without even asking, that he had nothing to do with the bodies. Leandro heard him confessing to growing marijuana and talking about bodies, and told him to shut up. Ricardo kept running his mouth. This was going to be too easy. Alfonso confirmed that that these were two of the men that had been arrested, along with Riviera for assaulting and raping Mei.

Carlos took Ricardo over to his truck, and advised him of his legal rights. Ricardo said, "I grow and sell marijuana. That's all I do. I never killed anyone. Leandro gets off on killing people."

Carlos asked, "How many people are out there in the graveyard? Did you help bury them?"

Continuin' On

"There are five women out there and one guy. I helped carry them and bury them, but I never killed anyone. You gotta believe me. I swear on my mother's grave. I even helped save a Chinese woman one night on the beach. They wanted to kill her, and I told them not to, and she managed to run away."

Carlos asked, "What's their nationality? Where are they from?"

"They're all Chinese, except for two Filipinas and one Japanese."

Carlos said, "There are only four graves out there. Where's the other two?"

He said, "Two of the graves have two bodies each. One's got a Chinese couple. They were killed for money and the girl was raped, even after she died. The other grave has a Japanese girl and a Chinese girl. The guys wanted to find out who fucked better, the Chinese or the Japanese." We were dealing with some sick perps.

In the over-head light of the truck cab, Fred helped Ricardo write out and sign his confession. He finally admitted that he had had sex with all the females, including Mei at the beach. Alfonso has taken Leandro away out of sight, and handcuffed him around a mango tree. The commissioner arrived, and we gave her the details. She decided to interview Leandro later. She said, "Let the bastard stew for awhile. He'll want to save his own ass in a few hours." She had sandwiches and coffee. Bless her soul. It was now well past midnight.

Alfonso and Fred transported both the suspects to the jail, and kept them separated. Lois had Ricardo placed in a secure cell. She wanted him to be alive for the trial. Ricardo gave the investigators six other names to talk to about the rapes and murders.

The names were well known on the police blotters: Jose Sumang, Arturo Taigeras, Marvin Arguero, Gerardo Cura, Jack Fernandez, and the ringleader Juan Riviera. Besides being involved in these murders, they had all raped Mei except for Fernandez. He had been in jail at the time. I had only been on island for about fifteen months, and I recognized the names from the newspapers and the nightly television news.

Lois issued a "no-exit" order at the airport and seaport for the additional suspects. She told the detectives not to allow the arrested suspects to make any phone calls before they could notify the other bad guys. She had the red Toyota pickup impounded for evidence processing.

Lois called up her best, most honest detectives, and briefed them on the new names in the investigation. She wanted all the named suspects arrested on probable cause for rape and murder, and marijuana cultivation.

As the sun rose, we finished up our reports and roped off a square kilometer area for further investigation. The FBI forensics crew notified Lois that they would be on scene in about four hours. After calling Cocina, I did what I do best. I lay down on a pile of palm fronds under a mango tree and fell fast asleep. Chuck was already snoring away. Lois had everything under control. It had quit raining.

17

DIGGING UP THE BODIES

The FBI sent a seasoned crew of agents and technicians from Hawaii for the crime scene work. Two of the agents had assisted in exhuming the dead bodies from the mass graves in Kosovo. The photographer in the group took dozens of photos just as Carlos had done. The team wanted to be able to present the court with photos of the scene as the work began. The agent sketcher then drew up the scene with measurements, as to where the graves were located in relation to the mango trees and the farm shed.

The team started at the grave where the skull was missing. Ricardo had drawn a rough sketch as to who was in each grave. The investigators decided to do the single graves first. The team approached the job as an archeologist would at an ancient historical site. They were methodical and took more photos as they progressed. They were looking for any minute evidence, items as small as fibers and hairs, and any dried fluids on the bodies, maybe a trace of semen.

The second grave was another female, probably a Filipina. I

watched and worried. I wondered which one would be Dina. I was happy that Cocina didn't have to witness the grave site exhumation. I was bordering on rage, and knew though experience, not to let emotions overwhelm good sense. Carlos walked over and patted me on the back. He said, "At least we'll know for sure. Cocina's family will have some closure."

I nodded and said, "The assholes. We need to have the death penalty in the islands. The old ways were good. Kill them with rocks, and drop them over the reef for the sharks." Carlos continued patting me on the back. Good *amigo*.

The team realized their limits for daylight, and tried to stay within a two hours limit for each exhumation to finish up before dark. The third grave was the Chinese couple. The fourth grave contained the Chinese and Japanese females. The rain was holding off. It was nasty, grisly work. Slow and methodical.

All of the victims were naked, with no jewelry or clear markings on the remaining skin. The Japanese female appeared to have an illegible tattoo on her right buttocks. The Chinese woman, in the grave with the man, had a possible, large birthmark on her right side. The bodies were in advanced degrees of decomposition. The team worked with masks and protective gear, and once the dirt was removed, the odor was unmistakable as decaying flesh. The team worked as though none of this mattered. They had experienced the gases and odors before, and were true professionals. When parts of the body seemed to move, they just shooed away the bugs and worms. The bodies were respectfully removed from the dirt, and were placed in large plastic bags for transport to the morgue and an autopsy. It appeared to the technicians that each skull had been bashed in with blunt object.

There was a fire pit nearby, and some parts of clothing, hats

Continuin' On

and shoes had been burned. Carlos and I took photos of this area, and placed the remaining, unburned pieces in evidence bags. We also retrieved some female clothing from the farm shed. The dumb shits had left some costume jewelry laying on the bench where they prepared the marijuana for sale. In a quick glance, it appeared that some of the flat jewelry had visible fingerprints. We saved these items for the crime lab processing. There was also some large wooden clubs in the shed, one of which had hair in the bark. Another had been carved smooth, and there were several identifiable prints on the handle, maybe blood.

All eight suspects in the case had fingerprints on file from previous arrests. A few match-ups would be fundamental.

The forensic crew worked until dark, and Lois secured the whole area with uniformed guards. Carlos and I headed home for the Beach Hotel, and a shower and a huge meal. After the threats on his life in previous cases, Carlos had moved into the hotel and never left. He had married Daisy and she had moved in too, just a few doors down from our penthouse.

I gave Cocina and the children an update. I couldn't say for sure if Dina had been in one of the graves. We would have to wait for the autopsy and investigation reports. Cocina just kept shaking her head, and muttered, "The bastards."

Carlos and I were back at the marijuana site at daybreak. After taking photographs and a dozen samples from different plants, Lois put the officers to work with their machetes and shovels. She let the press in for the photo op. The final count was eleven hundred mature plants, and hundreds of seedlings. The officers made a massive pile of plants, threw on some gasoline, and did a major burn. We didn't dare stand downwind in the heavy smoke. It would have been a cheap high, but we might have started wobbling and giggling, and got hunger pangs for beer and snacks. Not good in front of the media or driving down the mountain.

Lois coordinated the arrests of the remaining six suspects: Riviera, Sumang, Taigeras, Arguero, Cura and Fernandez. They were all in jail within twenty-four hours and placed in separate cells. Let the interrogations begin. Leandro had refused to talk to the investigators after being advised of his legal rights. He was arraigned and lawyered up with a public defender. Ricardo continued to play sweet music with his information. There was no stopping his chattering, and all his snitching was paying off for the investigators and prosecutors.

The results came in on the skull carried by the tiger. It was not Dina. It would be about three weeks before the FBI got back with positive identification on the other five victims.

Meanwhile, the court ordered that blood, fingerprint, urine, and hair samples be taken from the suspects for comparison.

18

BUTCH SOLVES ID THEFT CASE

Identity theft has become a major problem throughout the world. This computer-age theft topped the annual list of fraud complaints to the US Federal Trade Commission. Nearly twelve per cent or twenty-seven million people report that they had become a victim of some type of identity theft in the last five years. It is a major "white collar" crime.

Right after reading the latest crime stats, we received our first identity theft complaint at our Investigations Agency in early spring. Gloria Francisco had received her monthly credit card bill for nearly nine thousand dollars. Since she hadn't used the card for several months, it caught her attention big-time. She called the bank on Guam, and they seemed less than attentive, and said that they would refer her complaint to their investigators. Three weeks went by and no word from the bank. The next day, she received an overdue notice in the mail and was told that her interest percentage amount was being increased, and the bank assessed her a fifty dollar late fee. She also knew that a late payment would be recorded on her perfect credit report.

Gloria called the bank again. They told her not worry, that everything would be taken care of. We've all heard this before. Smile, don't worry.

This lackadaisical attitude irritated her to no end. She prided herself in being an upstanding citizen and wanted to do what was right. She was concerned that all her financial information was in the hands of a thief. She also knew that many times the credit card companies absorbed the loss, and passed on the expenses to other card holders. Gloria didn't like the immorality or the violation of any laws.

Carlos took the complaint and explained our investigation charges. She said that the local police were useless, and didn't understand the basic rudiments of using a computer for investigations. Gloria didn't balk at our fees. She wanted the whole mess cleared up. She gave us all her financial information and authorization letters for the bank and all her credit card companies. She had done the necessary work of canceling out her old cards, so there was no danger of new misuse, at least on her old cards.

We quickly found out that Gloria was well off, and had received a large insurance settlement when her husband was killed in a bus accident. Her credit report was perfect, as she had said. Plus, she owed zero in her bills, except for the standard monthly utility and food expenses.

Carlos ran into a dead end with his computer work. I kidded him, "Hey computer whiz kid. After all your classes, I figured you would have solved this one by now."

He smiled and said, "I'm getting nowhere. Maybe I should take the case to Cocina or Butch at the computer store?"

Continuin' On

I said, "Cocina has her month-end bills to reconcile. Let's hire Butch. He'll figure it out, knowing that guy. I think he went to Harvard with Bill Gates."

Carlos gave the case to Butch after one of our mountain hikes. We weren't concerned about confidentiality. Butch had dozens of high power clients, and never a word was leaked about their finances.

Butch said, "Give me a couple of weeks. The charges have been stopped, so there isn't a rush. You guys have to figure out if she lets someone use her card, or knows someone that has access to her information. I know the bank people. I can almost bet that there isn't some bullshit going on inside. They may be slow, but they're honest and reliable."

Butch was grinning, more than usual. I had to ask, "What the big smile about?"

"It just gives me a charge to know that you hotshot detectives have to come for help, especially to us computer techs."

"You got me Butch. Just keep your bill low." I waved good-bye.

He laughed and went back to work at the computer bench.

A month went by. Gloria was getting impatient. She dropped by the hotel every week, and I filled her up with optimism, and plenty of Starbuck Kenya coffee. Carlos just shook her head in amazement each time she left. He said, "She's got almost a million in the bank, and she's worried about a piddly nine thousand dollars."

I said, "Ain't the moolah mi amigo. It's the principle."

The next day, Gloria called and said that she had received two credit card bills on cards that she never applied for, or had received.

We learned that Gloria had a longtime house worker, Mila Bantu, who had been taking college classes in accounting. She knew all the bookkeeping and auditing computer programs. She had access to all of Gloria's personal data. Without notification to anyone, she had recently packed up and returned to Bangladesh. We verified that she had left by checking the airport records.

Butch called the next day. He said, "I know what happened. There's a definite pattern." He popped over to the hotel for a cold beer and a plate of *lumpia* egg rolls. Before he started, we filled him in on the possibility of Mila's involvement.

Butch said, "It all falls into place. You'll have to check the bank's cameras, and all the messages on Gloria's computer. I do believe you'll find a flurry of activity in the last few months. Mila probably got the new cards by internet, and everything that she bought probably went to Gloria's mailbox. Who better than Mila to handle the mail and take care of daily household chores? She probably was pretty good at forging Gloria's signature after all these years."

Butch continued, "I put a block on any application of any kind for Gloria Francisco. What this means is that any time there's a report or application, Gloria has to be contacted personally. No more cards or purchases on the internet. If Mila has left, then Gloria's problems are probably finished, except maybe for applications through Bangladesh. It's all a hassle. You can imagine the frustration and anxiety that a person goes through if the offender is still in the country." Victims now spend an average of six hundred hours recovering from the crime of identity theft, often over a period of years. Three years ago the average was one hundred and seventy-five hours of time, representing an increase of about two hundred and fifty per cent.

Continuin' On

I asked, "What should we be doing?"

He said, "Have the police get a warrant for her arrest and let immigration know. If she wants to come back to Saipan, let her come and arrest her at the point of entry. There's plenty of evidence right now for a warrant. I'll put the case together from the computer side."

Carlos said, "About half of the forgery and embezzlement cases involve the trusted employee. Usually a little old grandmother with false teeth."

Butch replied, "It seems to be the modus operandi. Any respectable company knows that you have to do periodic internal audits. But that concept hasn't caught on here, so the opportunity is just too tempting for people making minimum level wages."

We gave a full report to Gloria and she happily paid our bill. I told her that she was in the cash-and-carry or money order mode for the next few years. No more credit cards for awhile.

She smiled and said, "Maybe that's good. When I see a "sale" sign, I'm as bad as a college kid with the first credit card."

That brought back memories.

I knew about that problem when my daughter from my first marriage went off to college and ran up a huge debt, buying "necessities" such as televisions, walkman, laptops, the latest disk players, and one hundred dollar dinners at the seashore. And now I had my new daughter, Annie, about ready to go to California for her military science program. Oh, *ay naku.*

19

MWARS-MWARS AND PONYTAILS

Mercedes Santiago was a fine young woman whose luck had gone sour. She and Cocina had come to Saipan about the same time, and knew each other in elementary school in the Philippines. Although she was a skilled worker, the downturn of the island economy resulted in her and other foreign workers being laid off. She had forty-five days to find a job or go home, but there were no jobs. About a month into her time limitation, a neighborhood friend Felipe Zepeda asked her to marry him. Felipe was an old, fat man, but he had a kind heart and some income, and was a US citizen. She didn't want to go home to Bicol in the Philippines. The economy was even worse in that entire area, with thousands of people struggling to survive. She agreed to marry, and wasn't worried about the physical intimacy in the relationship. She had been married before, and had had one long-term boyfriend, as well as an aging lover on a sporadic basis. Knowing about men, and recognizing that Felipe was weak, she didn't feel that her new husband would be over-demanding in the bedroom.

Continuin' On

George and Jo set them up with an economy wedding, and I gave them the hotel wedding chapel for the ceremony. Guangman couldn't help himself and presented them with a nice sit-down dinner for fifty. The bride wore a new dress of a red flower pattern designed by Kaylene Mendoza of The Saipan Cowboy, our hotel tailoring shop. The groom wore a matching aloha shirt, and wore his hair in a long ponytail, Chamorro style. Mercedes also wore her hair in a ponytail, interwoven with flowers, but much shorter than Felipe's fine doo.

Both wore *mwar-mwars* woven with poinsettias and plumerias. It was a very impressive wedding, again with music by the Beachologist, Fred Cannon, and his musicians and hula dancers. Fred had taught his Chinese wife Miss Mae to do the island dances. She had the natural moves and moved her booty right along with the locals. The little group had their own T-shirts now that read, "Live a musical life. Pass it on."

Felipe and Mercedes settled into a routine marriage. Felipe gained a few pounds from Mercedes' Asian cooking, and started to look healthier. He was even seen exercising at the beach. Some of the guys couldn't help commenting that Felipe had to stay in good shape to satisfy his young bride. Mercedes obtained her spouse immigration status and was no longer threatened by deportation.

Felipe came from a large island family. Many of the members in the family were concerned that Mercedes was a gold-digger, and after Felipe's land holdings. They were unreasonably suspicious of her intentions, and several times, the female members of the family attacked her verbally at family fiestas. They never gave up criticizing her, and talking salaciously behind her back. She because increasingly frightened that they might assault her physically. Even women outside the family were particularly vocal, and didn't like the idea of a Filipina marrying one of their Chamorro men. One of the larger ladies actually bumped her in the public market, and said, "Get off our island, you *puta*!"

Felipe and Mercedes talked about it at length. Mercedes offered to sign an agreement that she would not take Zepeda land from the family. Felipe told her not to worry. Because of their special intimacy in handling a mutual problem, they made noisy physical love that night for several hours. Felipe climaxed, smiled, and rolled off Mercedes. He suddenly gasped for air, made a gurgling sound, and fell to the tile floor, hitting his head on an end bedroom table. Mercedes checked him for his vital signs. There were none. Mercedes' mind went into double-time, and quickly realized this was not a good situation for her. She saw the large bump and cut on his head, and panicked. The police and family would immediately decide that she had bludgeoned her old husband to death.

Mercedes knew that she had to get away to safety in the Philippines. She checked Felipe again, and knew that he was definitely dead. She grabbed her passport, her jewelry, and several thousand dollars that Felipe kept under a carpet. She got to the airport in time to make the direct flight to Manila. She wrote a letter of explanation about Felipe's death, and left the note with a TSA agent who promised to deliver it to Cocina at the Beach Hotel.

Cocina got the note next morning when the agent got off-duty. She read it, told me, and I called the police. As Mercedes had predicted, the police assumed that Mercedes had beat the old husband to death, even before they obtained the autopsy report. The pathologist at the hospital declared the death to be caused by a massive heart attack, and that the bump on Felipe's head had not been life-threatening. There was no indication of foul play.

Cocina tried calling Mercedes in the Philippines. She was not wanted by the authorities, and she could safety re-enter the CNMI based on her status as a widow. Her family was evasive abut her whereabouts except to say that she had retreated to the mountains of Bicol and Naga. This area is well-known as one of the last strongholds of the New People's Army, a leftover bunch of communists that financed their living expenses, and ammunition and weapons through robberies and kidnappings.

Upon hearing the latest, Carlos said, "I suppose now we have to go find her."

Cocina said, "Would you? Mercedes is a good soul, and deserves to know the news."

I knew the commies in that area had made statements that they would kill the first American they saw. I reminded Carlos that he was an American, and that the Muslim terrorists had just beheaded a Filipino-American near Jolo Island. I said, "And besides, Mercedes might not believe us. Might think it's a trap to get her back to Saipan. She knows we're former police and private investigators."

Carlos said, "Not to worry. Naga is safe. We fly in there, and hire some tough little Filipinos to go find her in the hills. They can bring her to us our hotel in Naga."

Cocina added, "I'll write a letter to her, and make several copies. She knows my writing, and that I would not betray her."

"Okay, we're off to the Philippines again. Always ready for my manicure, foot spa and pedicure, and deep massage."

Cocina grinned, "No massages with happy endings for you, Big Fellow. I will drain you before you leave Saipan. You will have to limp to the plane."

I replied, "Promises, promises."

I looked at Carlos and said, "Appears that I'll be busy for several hours evaluating the specific, scientific benefits of massage to the human body. See ya tomorrow at breakfast and then off to the airport."

Carlos said, "Research is important. Daisy will be home in about an hour."

Next morning, we flew to Manila, and then southward to Naga. I had three police contacts in PI, and they put me in touch with several experienced private investigators. Private investigators and the police are often one of the same in the PI, so the resources of the National Police Force would probably be used in finding Mercedes and hauling her safely back to Naga. A few extra pesos would speed up the search.

Two of the investigators looked good to us, Tommy Rivera and Eddie Gozalo. They were tough little dudes, and seemed to know how to get the job done. Tommy was still on the force, and Eddie had decided to retire, as he put it "because my bosses and I seemed to disagree on some civil rights issues." We later learned that Eddie had nearly killed a dope dealer for information. The investigation and the dealer's confession resulted in nearly three tons of marijuana and thousands of *shabu* pills being taken off the streets, but the case failed to meet court standards. The dopers walked free; and Eddie was told to retire.

We gave Eddie and Tommy all of the information on Mercedes, including her photos and the letter from Cocina. Eddie said that they would make some contacts around town and in some nearby villages, and get back to us. The lads didn't seem worried about the NPA. Tommy said, "If they fuck with us, we'll bring the wrath

Continuin' On

of the National Police down on their worthless souls. They know it too. We killed about ten of the fools about two months ago on a raid to free up a captured American held for ransom. We got the American okay, but we lost an officer and one other hostage. Goes with the territory. This is a dangerous game."

I said, "Salamat po. Appreciate your help. Stay in touch, and believe me, we will help in any way that we can."

Eddie said, "Just be ready to get out of town when we find the girl. See ya in a couple days. Adios." And off they went.

I looked at Carlos and smiled, "Is it time for our manicure and maybe a massage."

He said, "Let your conscience be your guide. And think machete on the home front."

We had fun walking around Naga. We were strangers in town, and a tourist novelty. Little children would run up to us, take our hands and press them to their foreheads as a gesture of honor and respect. The hawkers tried to pull us into their "sneaky-peeky" bars, and wanted us to check out their girls. Walking down some of the creepy alleys would be like a suicide mission for a clunk on the head or if *lango* enough, a definite possibility of AIDS or a STD. We stayed cool.

We hadn't heard anything from our investigators in over two days. I went to the corner market to refill our San Miguel beer cooler and to find some *shao bao*. When I walked up our hotel stairs, I heard a loud voice say, "You're coming with us, pendejo."

Equally loud and very determinate, Carlos boomed out, "You got it wrong. If you leave now, I won't hurt you little pukes."

I quietly walked to the open door. There were three of them, two with machetes, and one with a revolver. One of the clowns yelled, "Shoot his ass." Carlos saw me entering, and did a crazy man act, and started doing jumping jacks. The distraction worked. They didn't hear or see me. I took out the first guy along his head with a twelve-pack of beer, and managed to cripple another guy with a rolling knee tackle. Carlos grabbed the guy with the gun and knocked the gun off into a corner. He rushed the gunman and pushed him through the plate glass sliding door, and over the balcony. He fell down from the third floor in a sickening thud. There was little give to the concrete below. The other guy with the busted knees managed to stumble out the front door and disappear down the steps.

The third jerk regained consciousness, and wasn't sure what the hell was going on. He pretended to know only Tagalog but when Carlos tweaked his nose several times with the tip of his fingers, he decided it would be best to know a little English. To convince him farther, Carlos stepped on his bare feet with his army boots. English came flying out. He said that Eddie and Tommy had been checking around in his village for Mercedes, and their little cooked trio figured the Americanos would have money in their hotel room for a ransom payment. It appeared that the attack wasn't NPA motivated, but just a stupid robbery.

We reminded the little jerk that if he started flapping his jaws, we would tell the NPA that he was moving into their territory. His eyes went full open. He knew that he was in deep *ca-ca*. He stuttered, "If you let me go, I won't say a word. I'll even help you find the girl. I think I know where she is."

The police arrived to investigate the noise and commotion, and the dead body over the side. They knew that Eddie and Tommy were working with us. The older officer said, "Looks like a suicide. He must have been using drugs." He winked.

Continuin' On

Carlos went with it, and said, "For whatever reason, he just ran through the glass door and jumped. Too many drugs, I guess." Carlos handed the officer the gunman's revolver.

The little jerk added, "Yeah, that's right. That guy had been acting crazy and was out of control. He's a druggie."

The older officer said, "You want something done with this little ladrone? All these guys are nothing but trouble in the neighborhood. The guy that committed suicide has been arrested about ten times."

I said, 'No, he can go. He promised to help us find the missing girl."

My cell phone rang. It was Eddie. He said, "We got her. She's related to one of the NPA higher-ups, and he brought her to us when he heard the gossip. You owe us fifty thousand pesos for her release. When he found out that she was legal on Saipan, and that she wanted to go, he gave us permission to bring her to you."

"How long before you get here?"

Eddie said, "About an hour. Check the flight schedule. There should be a flight to Manila in about three hours. Buy the tickets."

"Good for you guys. We'll be packed and ready."

The older officer smiled. "We'll give you an escort to the airport. Meanwhile, you can buy us some lunch. *Crispy pata baboy* is on special today at the diner."

Carlos added, "But first get this little jerk in the wind. I don't like his face, and we're not buying him lunch." The officer gave a little gesture of approval with his head. The jerk took the hint and disappeared faster than the other miscreant who had stumbled down the stairway.

The lunch was excellent and the price right. I love the

Philippines. There is always a surprise and bargain around every corner, and every traveler in the PI knows that anything is possible, especially in Manila.

Mercedes arrived right on time after lunch. She was ecstatic and ready to get back to Saipan. She had hooked up with an old high school boyfriend in the mountains, but knew after a few days, that a long-term romance was hopeless. She was real tired of dirt floors and living by candlelight. We gave the police officers a nice reward for their assistance, and doubled the pay for our investigators.

The ride back to Saipan was routine. We had done our last minute shopping and found unique and different presents for everyone, just to ensure our hero's welcome back at the Beach Hotel. Cocina was happy to see Mercedes return to the island, and fixed her up with a special shared hotel room. She also had a job for her in the laundry section.

Carlos and I strolled down to the Beach Bar. The moon was full and reflected off the quiet lagoon. The sea was glimmering in silver. The swaying palms were silhouetted against the horizon. There was a warm balmy breeze that slightly stirred the orchids.

Carlos said, "Thanx for saving my ass back there. I think the little punk would have shot me. I had a real case of the nonepinephrines and cortisol. I could feel the chemicals surging through every pore in my body. I knew that I was in real trouble. He was all fucked-up on drugs and losing face."

I said, "It's only fair. You saved my butt on Mount Tapochau with that guy trying to knife me, and you saved little George in the cave. We make a good team."

"Tom, made me think. I have Daisy now and a baby. I could have died and lost it all."

Continuin' On

"First of all mi amigo, we're all going to die. We learn to manage fear. No one gets out alive. We just don't wanna rush it. We've got something special in the way we work together. You watch my back, and I will always be your cover."

He grinned and said, "Gracias, amigo. I will always be there for you."

"I never had any doubt. *Banzai*." Carlos and I had worked around danger and death for many years, and we had learned to adapt and deploy by using our knowledge and skills, and to survive. That's who we were, and we recognized that in each other.

Guangman brought us another round of warm *sake* to go with our fresh fruit.

20

NEW BBQ STAND

On our return to Saipan, we got some big news. Life on the islands can become wonderfully routine and almost boring at time. Yet, sex and romance are always cooking because of the heat and humidity, and the gorgeous sunsets. That excitement is followed closely by gossiping about the love entanglements, and whose doing what to whom.

But the *grande* news involved the new BBQ stand just down the street from the hotel. No one, and I mean no one, can barbeque like the islanders. The cooker usually marinates and seasons the meat, and then barbeques it on a skewer. Sometimes the cooker places peppers and other vegetables on the skewer with the meat. The closest stand had been about ten kilometers away, and with the price of fuel, that was a long way to travel on such a tiny island, especially when you got the munchies. Everyone at the hotel was ready to spend some bucks and get some tasty snacks.

When we saw the "Grand Opening" sign go up on the new stand, it became real. It was no longer a rumor, it was hap-

Continuin' On

pening. If you live on our island, you have either BBQ pork, fish and seafood, chicken or beef to choose from. And if the supply ships don't come in, or the fishing is bad, then you're stuck with canned meat of mysterious colors and unknown consistencies. The big day came for the opening and we were lined up, with saliva ready to drip on our chins. Even the neighborhood dogs and cats were milling about.

But alas, the stand did not open. The saleslady simply said, shrugging her shoulders, "No one brought the *tangan-tangan* wood for the fire. Maybe tomorrow." I asked why they didn't use dried coconut shells for barbequing, like they do all over Micronesia. She shrugged again. She was a very competent shoulder shrugger.

We had heard that these family members were champions with the BBQ, so we were there the next day, coming an hour late, so they would time to get the fire going. This time the saleslady said, "No one brought the meat. We had a little in the freezer, but someone ate it. Maybe tomorrow we open—come back, okay?"

We were unable to go for BBQ for the next three days. The hotel was full, and Carlos and I had to serve some legal documents for the island attorneys. We heard through the coconut express that the wood, fire, meat and BBQ sauce were ready, and the first skewers of meat were outrageously delicious. Some of our neighbors had been there, and were served superb food, and the drinks were actually ice cold.

Needless to say with the weekend upon us, the family and neighbors were hungry and ready for BBQ. This time, we went two hours late, giving the saleslady and cooker time to start the fire and find some meat. As we rolled up, we noticed the "Grand

Opening" sign was gone, but happily we saw smoke coming from the rear of the building. It had to be BBQ, and we were ready. We even brought our own bottle of Mexican hot sauce to spice up the meat.

When we looked closer, there was a home-made sign on the front door, which read, "Gone to a funeral on Tinian—will be back in 1-2 weeks." The smoke that we had seen was coming from a trash fire in back. A handyman was tending the fire, and we asked when the owners were coming back. He said that he didn't know, but it wouldn't be any time soon. He said the BBQ sales had been slow, so the family wasn't enthused about coming back from the funeral.

I told him that we had tried to buy BBQ. He nodded. I asked him if he had ever had any BBQ from the stand. He said, "Only if I make it, but I usually can't find any wood or meat." He added that oftentimes the owner would rather go fishing or play poker than tend to the BBQ stand. "The owner is a great cook, but lacks a true business sense," he said, raising his eyebrows.

We never did get any food from the new stand, still driving ten kilometers up north for our BBQ. Many nights we just settled for some hors d'oeuvres, Hawaiian pu-pus, out by the pool.

I saw the owner several weeks later, and asked what had happened with the stand. He explained that it was a lot of work, and people expected you to be there all the time, and his relatives were always taking his meat and wood. He further added, "There's not much profit in BBQ."

As I drove away, I couldn't help thinking, "No BBQ to sell, no money coming in, stored closed…hmmm" Yeah, he was right—no money in BBQ.

The following month the family went to Tinian to stay. As

Continuin' On

with any abandoned building in the islands, the stand was soon dismantled piece by piece. After about two weeks, there was only a cement slab left. Islanders feel that if no one is using it, they must not want it.

Recycling at its best.

21

MANGKUKULAM VISITS MARY

I would venture to say that there virtually isn't one person from the Philippines that doesn't believe in ghosts and witches, and black magic. I purposefully and distinctly include college educated people and Filipinos who live in other countries, and have been away from home for a long time. They still pin people up on crosses, representing the crucifixion. You must remember that open heart surgery is still done theoretically without instruments or blood loss in the Philippines, simply by reaching through the breastplate, removing the heart, and providing a massage. Cancer can be cured with special blends of dried leaves mixed with ashes from a fire. People believe this stuff. And even if the child is *halfa-halfa*, that is only half Filipino mixed with another racial extraction, the belief will still be there. These superstitions aren't going away any time soon. Ancient legends, gods and ghosts linger in their everyday lives.

A lot of the beliefs probably came along from the early tribal ceremonies, layered over with the bells and incense, and the

Continuin' On

speaking of foreign languages, sounding like mumbo-jumbo to the first peoples to meet the priests and the mullahs. Up north in the Philippines, Christianity adjusted well into the local life, and vice-versa. Down south, Islam fit in, and came from neighboring Malaysia.

Cocina had a first cousin, Mary Alcantara, living just a few blocks from the hotel. She had been distressed and worried about Dina, just like the other members of the family. She and Dina had grown up together like sisters. She was first in line to contribute blood for DNA testing to build the family profile to compare with any victim that might be found.

She would often go to church and the shrines, to pray for Dina. She lit hundreds of candles for Dina in the religious centers. Cocina was worried that she was becoming too intense and tried to get her more involved with our family so she would think of something other than Dina. Mary came over for dinner and played with the children.

After leaving our penthouse on a particularly clear night, Mary was overtaken from behind by a whirling sound. She looked up and saw a *mangkukulam* hovering just over a coconut tree. The witch was dressed in black and seemed to be floating on air. It was a female with long, black flowing hair. She wasn't on a broomstick like in the fairy tales. Mary was relaxed, and didn't panic because she had been taught that some witches are good, not intending to hurt you. Mary knew that if this witch had been bad, she would have been attacked or dead by now. There were no other witnesses that night.

The witch spoke in *Tagalog*, the second official language in the Philippines. She said, "*Mabuhay*, Mary. I know you."

Mary answered and asked, "Why do you know me?"

The witch said, "Because I have heard you praying to God about your cousin, Dina."

Mary said, "Have you been following me? Why do you care?"

"Because I saw your cousin murdered, and I didn't have the powers to stop it. They were very evil men. She was killed up in the mountains and then buried. She only suffered for a little while. Dina was a good girl, and has gone to join Jesus in heaven."

"So Dina is okay now? She's happy?"

The witch answered, "Yes, Dina's spirit is alive and well. You don't need to worry anymore."

"I'm so glad to hear that. How about the evil men?"

"I can't do anything to them directly, but I did little things like giving them flat tires, snapping the water lines to their houses and making them lose at poker. I also helped the tiger find the graves by riding on his back and steering him to Dina."

Mary said, "*Salamat po.*"

"You go home and be content. Goodbye."

With a flash of light and a gust of wind, the witch disappeared. Mary's worries slid off her shoulder and she skipped on home. She had wonderful, pleasant dreams that night. She was so relieved.

When the family gathered for coffee at the hotel the next morning, Mary told her story. The family members smiled and laughed, believing that Dina had sent a good witch to tell us that she had gone to heaven. The family believed every word. Cocina glanced over at me and said, "It'll be fine now. We'll get those *animales* convicted, and move on with our lives. We'll think of Dina every day, and if I know her, we better remember her birthday, or we can expect some crazy tricks."

Continuin' On

I nodded in agreement. Cocina said, "Let's light some more candles for Dina."

Carlos and I made eye contact. He raised his eyebrows. I scratched my head. Chinese Daisy gave us a bewildered look, wondering what Buddha would say. We lit several candles at the Mother Mary Shrine near the hotel's wedding chapel.

Strong beliefs can make things happen. The horror of Dina's death was no longer the governing factor in our thoughts. Dina's afterlife was. She was happy and safe.

Perception and belief are as real as the actual event.

22

THE SUNKEN NUESTA SENORA DE LA CONCEPTION

Raoul Russell of Angel's Camp, California, came to us at the Investigation Agency with an unusual tale. He wanted our help in regaining certain pieces of treasure that been recovered from the sunken *Nuestra Senora de La Conception*. When Raoul's father Robert died recently of a heart attack, Raoul found an old IOU note in a box of his grandfather's possessions hidden away in a spare closet. His father had never told me about the old box. The IOU was for one thousand dollars dated November 4, 1911. The grandfather, Clancy Russell, received the money from Herberto Guerrero, and in turn, the grandfather had given twenty gold bracelets, twelve gold and silver rings, and ten gold necklaces to Herberto as collateral. Supposedly, the jewelry had come from the sunken ship. Also in the grandfather's box, there was a copy of the IOU note which was stamped "PAID IN FULL" dated March 31, 1917. No mention was made on any documents of the jewelry being

Continuin' On

returned to the grandfather.

Saipan has an extensive written and pictorial history of the sunken Spanish galleon in the CNMI Museum near the old Japanese civic center. The ship was the largest of the galleons that transported gold and silver, silks and special fibers, porcelain and perfumes, and other exotic goods from Manila to Acapulco. The ship carried over two thousand tons, and was sixty meters long. The captain was young and inexperienced, and as the ship neared Agingan Bay at the southern tip of Saipan, a vicious tropical storm crashed against the ship. Coupled with this natural phenomenon was a mutiny among the experienced officers aboard.

As a consequence on September 10, 1638, the ship hit the reef and was instantly destroyed by breaking in half. Of the four hundred crew and passengers, only twenty eight people survived. The captain perished with his ship. The treasures of the ship were spread over a wide area, and to this day, it is estimated that much of the treasure has not been recovered. There was not an accurate inventory in Manila or aboard, as some of the Spanish officials were smuggling valuable items back to Spain and weren't being good citizens in paying taxes or sharing the booty.

To this day, interesting items are rolling up on shore. After a recent storm, one of the ship's cannons washed up on shore in front of a major hotel. Divers have found intact clay vessels containing olive oil, water and wine. These vessels weighed up to eighty pounds, and the contents were still pure and potable. The occasional piece of gold or silver is still being found.

Raoul was not a poor man, and not in desperate need of gold. He was curious and creating a family history for his children. He wanted us to trace the IOU and jewelry back to the Guerrero Family, and to recover the gold if it rightfully belonged to the

Russell Estate. He left a decent retainer with Carlos. Raoul flew back to California and asked that we send periodic reports through email.

Carlos looked at me, and said, "What a country. Last month, we're chasing cattle rustlers, and then searching for murderers, and now tracing old records and looking for the loot from a sunken galleon."

I said, "Yo Carlos. That's why this job is exciting and so much fun. You never know from day to day."

"Yep, I'm loving it."

I said, "Where do we start with old records? The dates of the IOU go back to the German Colonial days. And we know the old records were either destroyed by typhoons, humidity or termites. Or maybe destroyed in the war."

"Let's go talk to the Guerroros. Maybe they've kept some records high and dry. It's a big family. We just have to figure where the lender, Herberto fits into everything."

Carlos and I headed over to the Guerrero's Store, and spoke to the manager, Henrietta Guerrero, who happened to be the great granddaughter to Herberto. She didn't know about any loans or gold jewelry, but had heard that the family had inherited some jewelry from the ship wreck. She also heard that the Japanese had confiscated all their valuables during World War II. She telephoned her grandfather, Jesus Guerrero, who agreed to come to the store.

Jesus was feeble, but his eyes were full of life. It's bullshit when the body breaks down, and the brain is still going full blast. He spoke broken English. He had been sent to school in Japan, and was fluent in both Japanese and Chamorro. Carlos did most of the talking. I did a lot of gesturing and smiling. He remembered

Continuin' On

the jewelry, and something about Clancy Russell paying back some money. The story had been told to him by his grandfather.

When his great grandfather, Herberto, died, the family didn't know what to do with the jewelry. Except for one elder son, they didn't know about any IOU with Clancy. So for about ten years, the ladies in the family wore the jewelry publicly. This was during the German times, and the Germans never confiscated anything from the families, except land and a portion of the crops from the farmers. When the Japanese seized the islands in 1914, they started an intensive program of agriculture and education, and didn't hesitate to seize anything of value. Some of the families lost the treasures from the ship to the Japanese officials.

The Guerreros sensed that they would lose the gold jewelry if they didn't hide it. What better place than Herberto's grave? And that's what they did, and no one was the wiser. The Japanese had not noticed or seen the gold on the Guerreros. Throughout the rest of the century, the jewelry apparently stayed in the grave. No one had the *cojones* to dig up the casket and use or sell the jewelry. It was considered disrespectful and might also free up some evil spirits.

Jesus made a few telephone calls to the older members of the family. None of these older folks had seen an IOU or knew Clancy, but all basically had the same story about hiding the gold from the Japanese, and then just leaving it in the grave. The newest generations knew nothing of the gold.

I explained what our employer from California was trying to do. I was looking for solutions in making a determination as to who owned the gold, and also should the gold just stay in the grave for eternity. Jesus called a family meeting for the following Saturday. He introduced me at the gathering. Carlos was right. It was a large family with about two hundred people in attendance. I told them about my client. After my presentation, Jesus asked Carlos and me to leave, so the family could decide what to do.

Jesus and Henrietta came to our office the next day. They knew about cops. It was a form of bribery and probably meant to soften us up. He was carrying a large box of fresh baked donuts. I built a fresh pot of Starbuck's, and we settled down to palaver. Carlos got the maple bars before I had a chance.

Jesus presented a plan that might work out for everyone. He said that the older members of the family had been curious for years about what and how much gold was in Herberto's casket. With court approval, they were willing to exhume the body. Any documents inside would be copied and given to anyone that wanted to see. If there was gold, it would be appraised by an independent firm, and then the value split as follows: 25 % for my client, 50 % to be divided among family members, and 25% would be contributed to the museum and college for historical purposes. However, this split only applied to the gold as described in the IOU. Any other valuables, which may have been hidden from the Japanese, would go directly to the Guerrero family with a formula for distribution.

I called Raoul in California and told him about the proposition. His response was, "I'm not looking for a lot of money. I want some answers, which will happen. The idea of contributing either the gold or some greenbacks to the museum and college makes really good sense to me. Got a good lawyer on island?"

I said, "Not a problem."

Rather than spending a fortune in legal fees, the Guerreros mutually agreed to a lawyer that I knew from my policing days in Los Angeles, Ernie Martines. He was respected in the local

Continuin' On

courts. He did an affidavit, signed by the parties, and presented it to the court. The judge issued an order authorizing the exhumation and also agreed to the split of the gold as set up by our investigations agency and the Guerrero family.

The funeral company came out two days later with their heavy equipment. The hole was carefully dug and the casket excavated. The box was made of fine mahogany, and had stood the ravishes of time fairly well, with very little rot. The interior of the casket was dry, and the body of Herberto Guerrero, in a mummified form, lay looking up at us. We anxiously checked around his body, and found bags of gold and what appeared to be rubies and diamonds. When anything of value was being hidden from the Japanese, the family members must have decided this was a good idea, and piled additional treasures inside. The shipwreck jewelry was in a cloth bag next to Herberto's head. An unsigned note was attached to the bag that said, "We're not sure who Clancy is, but father said he doesn't know where to return the jewelry. His debt is paid. We sent a copy of his IOU to his old address in California."

With three members of the Guerrero family, Carlos and I inventoried the items inside the casket. We made a long list with descriptions and took digital photos of the items. Carlos was still enjoying his new camera. Ernie Martines oversaw the whole process for his report to the court.

The family reburied Herberto with full reverence and appreciation. They placed a time capsule inside the casket, and a photo of every Guerrero member on Saipan. He was the big *kahuna*, and remembered by all the souls that traced their lives back to him, and his wife Alberta. There would be funding for all the children to follow their dreams and go to college or start their own businesses.

The value of the casket items far exceeded any of our expectations. There was both a market value assessed, and a historical, antique estimate. The items listed in the IOU were valued at well over four million dollars on the open market. Raoul and the Guerreros decided to send these items to the Sotheby's Auction House in New York, and eventually reaped over twice the amount. After the auctioneer and legal fees were paid, there were eight million dollars to be shared from the original plan.

It was the same situation with the other items hidden in the casket from the Japanese. The Guerreros created a foundation that would handle the monies for the family. The final accounting was about twelve million dollars for the additional items, plus another four million dollars from the shipwreck jewelry.

Raoul was satisfied in receiving his two million dollars. He gave a generous bonus to Carlos and me which we used for education investments for our children. The museum and college each received one million. Together, they very cleverly found an artist who was able to make almost exact copies of the jewelry for display in their galleries.

Wherever they might be, Herberto and Clancy must be smiling. The debt is paid, and the jewelry returned. Everyone is satisfied, and the offspring have tons of opportunities.

With my freewheeling imagination, I can go back in time and visualize some hard-working Japanese officer thinking, "I know those people have some gold and jewelry. I've heard the rumors. I wonder where they hid their treasures."

23

THE POSSE DECIDES TO PARTY

The Filipinas on Saipan are a very close-knit group. Cocina and her cousin Mary belonged to a covey of beautiful women who called themselves The Posse. The number in the group was usually about ten. They traveled like a gaggle of geese when they went shopping, working out at the gym, or taking college classes. They were supportive of one other. When one in the group got sick or needed someone to talk to about romance or job troubles, there would always be two or three of the ladies that could help out. About half of the members had husbands or boyfriends, while the other half was always on the hunt for a good mate. The committed ones, of course, were also looking out for their friends. There was always a lot of match-making and blind dates happening. Woe to the potential suitor who had not made the grade with someone in The Posse. Once you were out, you were out with the whole group. There was also an understanding in the group that there would be no hand-me-downs and no coming back if the suitor got dumped. Menage-a-trois and lesbianism were definite taboos.

Posse members Grace and Joanne were single ladies. They decided it was time to get Cocina and Mary out of the house, and cheer them up after the terrible things happened to Dina. Once they heard about the mangkukulam's visit and that Dina was in heaven, they decided the timing was right for a social gathering. They knew that Cocina and Mary liked to dance, so they talked them into going to the GIG discothèque on Friday night. They argued that Dina liked to dance and sing, so she would expect them to get out and enjoy the music. The justification was clear that girls gotta have some fun.

Finding the right partner for dancing on Saipan is never a problem, so long as the music is loud and modern. The music has to have a strong, booming beat, with the timing and sounds as definite as the throes of passion and lovemaking. The pulsating sounds are stored in the brains from the beginning of humankind itself. The rhythmic dance encouraged the fantasy of coupling, but with clothes on and in a vertical position, and socially acceptable. And of course, the ladies called their suggestive gyrations merely fun and exercise, and inwardly they knew that the moves meant more. Men saw the movements as potentially promising, and could almost hear the banging of headboards through their filtering system.

The ladies liked to let loose and dance, solo or together, or with *bakla* and cross-dressers. Sometimes a navy ship came in, and the lads were only too agreeable to hold hands and buy drinks. The dancing continued right until closing at 2AM. The committed ladies went for coffee or tea and then home, while the single gals followed the course wherever nature might take them. Some of the navy lads were quite persuasive, and in some cases, the liquor helped tip the scales.

Continuin' On

The husbands and boyfriends liked this plan. Not many adult men are into dancing. Friday night was pay-for-view Thai boxing night in the hotel conference room, coming direct from Bangkok. Dancing didn't start until about 10:00 o'clock, and the boxing an hour earlier. So the guys got comfortable in the padded, lounge chairs. The gals set them up with beers and chips, and I brought out a fresh box of special cigars from Bali. You could feel the testosterone taking effect after a few San Miguels and a maduro cigar. The boxing finished up the machismo rush.

The gals were all chuckling in the corner. I knew enough Tagalog to know that they thought we were very entertaining, as they watched the transition from ordinary guys into prideful lions. Grace and Joanne added to the fun by shaking their well-exercised gluteus maximus muscles as they were going through the exit door. The lads gave a hoot and holler. The gals swayed some more.

As Cocina was leaving my table, she said, "Tom-Kat, it just doesn't feel right, what with Dina not being identified yet. Think it's okay? I feel kinda guilty."

I said, "I would normally say, if something doesn't feel right, don't do it; but in this case, Dina has gone on, and she would want you and Mary to enjoy yourselves. I remember her well. In fact, if she was here, she'd be the one to organize the dancing posse."

"Well, I feel like having some fun, and burning up some calories on the dance floor." She hesitated and then said, "Okay. I'm going. The kids are all bedded down for the night. Not to worry."

I answered, "Yep, but don't have too much fun. I hear there's a ship in the harbor. Maybe I should worry about all those young, virile sailors."

"Like you have something to worry about, my strong, handsome man." She kissed me full on the lips, and the guys let out more hoots and hollers. I noticed several of the lads watching her "walk-away" sashay, but they were cool and didn't say anything to piss off her old man.

The fights on TV were good. Afterwards, we threw on some action movies and did some yelling and screaming for our heroes, and some booing for the villains. Fortunately the conference room was soundproof and didn't disturb the guests. Two Japanese male guests wandered by and joined in the fun. They didn't know a word of English, but were soon cheering the good guys on. Action movies require very few words, English, Martian, or Esperanto.

Guangman heard the ladies returning, and got the green tea boiling away. He brought out some freshly baked Korean pastries. The lads had settled down, and were now ready for an update from the disco dancing.

The gals walked in, giggling and talking again in Tagalog. They weren't *lango,* just happy and carefree. Out of the original group, I noticed that Grace and Joanne were missing.

Cocina said, "You girls stop it. Straighten up." They kept giggling and jostling one another. I heard something about two guys and licorice sticks, and liking the taste of licorice.

Cocina pulled me to the side and said, "You won't believe this but Grace and Joanne went to the hotel with two Afro-American sailors from the ship. Somewhere the posse had heard that a black guy's *chili* was called a licorice stick. That's what they're laughing about. Grace and Joanne are in for a "big" lesson of love."

I asked, "What kind of guys were they? Are they okay guys?" Females at night with strangers piqued my police instincts.

"Yeah, relax Papa. The guys sat with us all night, and we know their names and the ship is the USS Cagle. We know their hotel

Continuin' On

and room numbers. The girls have their friend Joyce at the front desk. I'm not worried about the girls. We ate too much but hardly did any drinking tonight. They have their cell phones and they can maneuver like crazy."

I said, "They're in for a big experience, but they're both mothers, so they should do okay in the *puki* area. Just to be safe, give the girls a call. Make Papa feel better."

Cocina called Grace, and she was fine and going to stay all night. Grace said that she would get to her accounting job by eight in the morning. Joanne was okay but very excited. Cocina said that she kept saying, "Holy shit! You won't believe it." She had already found her nirvana three times. She added that she was staying all night, and maybe the weekend. The ship didn't sail until Monday.

After tea and snacks, our group started to drift off. Carlos said, "Don't you characters be telling Daisy about licorice sticks. She might get interested."

I said, "Yeah, I know what you mean. But my little sweetie Cocina already heard about it. And she remembers Fancy Sandoval, our giant *hombre* from Chuuk.

She put her arm in mine, and whispered in my ear, pulling me to the stairs. I looked back at Carlos and said, "Cocina told me to remind you that it isn't the size that counts, it's the style and technique."

Carlos replied, "I hope that's true. I sure hope that's the gospel truth."

I waved goodnight to him as my lady pulled me up the stairs to the penthouse.

Carlos said, smiling, "Well just in case, don't tell Daisy anyway."

24

THE SUN-TANNED GIRLS

This was the second year that they showed up. There were seven young girls, early twenties maybe, and two older ladies that may have been chaperones or guards. Four of the girls were different than the ones last year. I hadn't seen the older women before. I usually was able to spot cops, and the older women were likely federal agents. I had no idea what was going on. They registered routinely, and used personal credit cards. The older ladies hovered over the girls, and were around them most of the day. Young men were discouraged to get too friendly.

They purported to be beach volleyball players, and we did have an island-wide tournament coming up. They didn't play volleyball last year. Through Cocina, I got to know the two older ladies, Roni Cooper and Ruby Walquist. Over coffee, I learned that the seven girls were on Saipan to compete in the tournament, and would stay at the Beach Hotel while working out and practicing. Ruby said, "We didn't compete last year. Just wanted to scope out the competition and see what our

Continuin' On

chances would be of taking home a trophy."

I said, "The girls look like they're fit and athletic, and they're already sun-tanned. Where are you from? They look like beauties from California."

Roni answered, "We're from all over the states. We did a lot of training before we came out, up north in San Jose."

I looked over at Cocina and asked, "Where did you put them?"

She said, "They're all side-by-side on the fourth floor, just like they requested. Two rooms have two girls each, another with three girls. Roni and Ruby are at the end of the hall. The girls have to walk by their room before they get to the elevator."

Ruby asked, "Are you a cop?"

"Nope, used to be. Now just a private investigator and a posadero."

"Do you have a firearm?"

"Yeah, just a .22 cal rifle and a 4/10 shotgun. But if you ever need immediate help, Carlos is just above your rooms. He has plenty of firepower, and linebacker shoulders."

I thought, "Interesting questions from a volleyball coach."

I watched the girls play sand volleyball on the beach in their skimpy matching red bikinis. It was good to see young people so carefree, untroubled and playful. They reminded me of *munquitas* from Mexico. I looked up at our penthouse balcony, and saw that our teenager, Anthony, was also enjoying the volleyball games and the players. I waved at him, and he went back inside. The boy was growing up.

After a few games, it was clear that the girls were not of championship material. They were having lots of laughs, and definitely had tight athletic rumps, but they would never win the competition. They would be lucky to move up one rung in the ladder, and then only if one of other teams failed to show up. Roni and Ruby worked with them and tried to coach. Roni was in good shape and appeared to know the game, but Ruby was another matter. She had developed the middle-age spread of a woman that had stopped exercising.

The volleyball girls never got past the "having fun" strategy. Roni was frustrated.

I overheard Ruby say, "Roni, relax. It's only for a few more weeks, and if the bad guys decide to settle, the job is done."

Roni replied, "You're right boss, just a few more weeks. But you know me. I like to win. It's so much sweeter than losing."

Cocina came by, and said to me, "Still helping the girls improve their game?"

"Yep, hard at work. I'm watching that girl in the red swimsuit."

"Well, do-gooder. Seven girls in red bikinis is a big job. Come on up to the penthouse for lunch. Guangman has fixed us a high-fiber, lo-calorie extravaganza."

I smiled, "I hate to leave my work." I jumped up and gave her a giant bear hug and a quasi-wet kiss, and we strolled over to the elevator. I said, "I bet the kiddies are going to be excited about all those veggies, and no fried food."

The girls also took a lunch break. After lunch, I usually take a short siesta or catch-up on my reading. Today, I got on the internet and searched for some of my old US Marshal compadres. Deputy Jim Worthington was easy to find in Los Angeles. Because of the time distance on the West Coast, he was off duty and enjoying his family. From several other sources and contacts, I got his home phone number and gave him a call.

We had been soccer dads for several years, and had become

Continuin' On

good friends. We did the catch-up on our lives and families, and he promised to bring his family out to Saipan on vacation. I asked him about the girls here at the hotel and their two guardians.

Jim said, "I can't talk about it. Looks like a deal might be coming down the turnpike any day soon."

"What kind of deal?"

"You think you're going to get your answers out of me in your casual, sneaky way? You gotta remember that we took the same interviewing classes at the academy."

Jim eventually admitted that he knew Roni and Ruby. He asked, "Is Roni driving you crazy yet? She's one of our up-and-comers. You can't slow that girl down. If I don't retire soon, she'll be my boss and trying to get me all motivated like a new recruit."

We talked some more about old times, and what his plans were on retirement. Before we hung up, he admitted the girls were in the Witness Protection Program and that Ruby and Roni were their care takers.

I strolled over to beach bar, and saw that three of the girls were heavily into afternoon umbrella drinks. Four young local lads were swarming all over them, like hungry tigers going in for the kill. I called Roni on the phone and told her that three of her charges were drunk in the bar, and that co-mingling was a strong possibility. She said that she would be right down.

I walked over the girls and said hello. One of the lads asked, "Hey Pops, what are you doing here?"

I introduced myself as the owner of the hotel, and the protector of all young ladies from the mainland. The mouth of the group got himself all puffed up, and told me, "Old man, go watch TV or do your crochet, or whatever you old farts do."

"Sorry, can't do that. Afternoon television sucks, and I lost my crochet needles." I was now feeling like the medieval knight ready to fight the dragons.

The lad's testosterone was bubbling from every pore. The Mouth had been challenged. Every male knows what follows next. Most guys would rather take a beating than lose face in front of their buddies. Throw in some alcohol and you have the makings of a typical bar fight.

One of the girls said, "I can't believe it. Guys are fighting over us. This is great!"

Another girl said, "Shut up, Louise. You know we're supposed to be low profile. You want us on the damn evening news and getting us killed?"

Mouth pushed me in the chest. I pushed back and moved into my police defensive position. I had learned to fight from my police training in weaponless techniques, and how to avoid being hit and injured. The moves require judo-like precision and using the other fighter's energy and thrusts for disabling his attacks. He jumped full blast into the fight, charging like a crazy bull. I simply stepped aside, and clipped him on the back of the head. He went down, crashing into a wooden wall.

As he started to get up, Guangman struck him hard on the back of the head, with the largest frying pan I'd ever seen. Mouth went unconscious. Two of the other dipshits decided to charge me, about the time Roni showed up with her pepper spray. She gave each guy two blasts from her canister, catching them in the eyes and noses. They were finished and begging for decontamination. Guangman took their hands and guided them to the sand. He gave them the water hose. He laughed and said in his broken English, "Don't worry. It stops hurting in two hours."

Hearing the commotion, Carlos stepped inside the bar.

Continuin' On

Mouth had become conscious. He knew Carlos as an elder in his village. Mouth and the other guy in the bar, who hadn't moved from his chair, apologized profusely.

Carlos glanced at me and said, "What do you want to do with these guys. I can call the area police car and have them hauled away."

I said, "No damage, no foul. Let their parents handle it, island-style."

Carlos said to Mouth, "Go get your two buddies off the beach, and get out of here. I will be letting your parents know. And get some jobs. Don't be drinking and playing the fool all day."

All four of the chumps came to me and apologized. I told them that they were banned from my hotel and bar for six months.

Roni scolded the three girls and sent them to their room. She reminded them that they had their first tournament game the next day.

I said to Roni, "It's coffee time." I told her about my contact with Deputy Marshal Jim Worthington. She liked Jim and had learned much of her job from him. She said that their Saipan assignment was probably going to end next week. Knowing she was single, I asked her if she had visited with George and Jo about their dating and marriage service. She said that she had thought about it, but just last night, her boyfriend had called and asked to get back together. She was going to give him another chance, and maybe adjust her long work hours.

Guangman came over and joined us. He said, "Pretty good, eh Boss? The way I got that guy."

I said, "A-1 good. Thanks. Where'd you get that giant pan?"

"Through E-bay, Boss. I love doing that bidding."

Next day, the girls managed to make a decent showing against the Japanese Team. They got a few points. Three of the girls were obviously in pain from their hangovers but they played hard to win. They eventually lost, and were introduced to bowing in respect, Japanese style.

The word came down later in the afternoon that a plea bargain had been reached and signed by the crime dons and their lawyers. The dons never knew about the girls' upcoming testimony in specifics, and the prosecutor showed the defense that all his evidence had been obtained in other areas. The dons expressed no animosity to the girls and their statements.

Roni and Ruby joined Cocina and me for a special coconut crab dinner. We finally got the details on the girls' involvement. They had all been cocktail waitresses and helpers in a New Jersey restaurant where the organized crime leaders had their lunches. Three of the girls also worked as evening escorts. The girls had overhead information about money laundering, different crime operations, and several hits on other crime figures muscling in on their territories.

Four of the girls had come forward because they had heard about the FBI informant fees. The other three provided information after their arrests for minor dope violations, prostitution and DUI. All charges would be dropped, and the girls would receive more reward money than they could earn in a year at waitressing. While hiding out, they had also enjoyed government-paid holidays in San Jose and Puerto Rico, and now on Saipan, courtesy of the Witness Protection Program and the American taxpayers. Due process and justice are never cheap.

On the following weekend, Deputy Marshals Ruby and Roni, and four of the girls boarded the Saturday afternoon flight and headed home to the mainland. Three of the girls decided to stay

Continuin' On

on-island, and use their hospitality skills in the tourist industry. Cocina hired the oldest girl Stephanie right away to work in our Beach Bar. She had watched Stephanie carefully, and knew that she had style and grace, and a very warm outgoing personality.

Cocina found me lying on the hammock near the beach. She said, "Whatsa doing? Thinking about your volleyball team?"

I pulled her over on top of me. "Nope, just watching the waves coming ashore, and listening to the birds chirping from the top of the palms.

"We've got a nice life here."

I smiled and said, "*Ichiban.* Mighty fine. The finest kind."

She cuddled closer.

25

IDENTIFICATION AND TRIAL

All the laboratory and investigation reports were combined, coordinated and double-checked. Dina was positively identified through DNA and dental charts and by some of the clothing and jewelry left in the marijuana shed. Pubic hairs belonging to Juan Rivera and Geraldo Cura were found on her body.

Whitey had found the skull belonging to the other Filipina, Eva Marquez, a well known "punchboard" from the local bars. The skull was matched up with Eva's body at the gravesite. She had been arrested numerous times for drunkenness and prostitution. She had eluded physical arrest several times by giving a free screw to the cops. The detectives were amazed that the defendants had killed her, because she was willing to fuck whoever happened along. She also sold marijuana for Juan Rivera. It was later learned through snitches that Eva had been skimming the profits from the weed. Bad form in the dope business.

The Japanese female and the Chinese female were both tourists who had gone missing. The Japanese was Masako

Continuin' On

Kobayashi and the Chinese was Sung Eui Lee. Both girls were in their late teens, and were off on vacation, carefree and wanting to see a tropical island. They disappeared on separate nights, and apparently didn't know each other before the abduction. According to Ricardo Zambales, Masako was kidnapped first and held in a cage at the marijuana field. Several of the defendants fucked her, and then Jack Fernandez came up with the bizarre idea of capturing a Chinese girl, and doing a comparison study as who had the smoothest pussy, and who could fuck the best for survival.

Sung was kidnapped the next night, and both girls were repeatedly raped, and held in cages. The defendants kept the girls alive for several days. Zambales admitted that he had fucked both girls. Their bodies were identified through family DNA testing, and dental charts brought from their home countries. Pubic hairs from six of the defendants were found on their bodies, including Zambales. When Fernandez was arrested, he was carrying photos and personal items belonging to Masako and Sung.

The Chinese couple in the grave were identified as Sami Lee and her husband, Yu Lim. Backtracking on their history, it was learned that they were business people looking for investments in the CNMI or Guam. They were carrying over fifty thousand US dollars. It was suspected by the FBI that they were researching ways of laundering illicit monies from China. They were linked to a larger powerful tong from Beijing. Zambales said the defendants had heard through their Chinese contacts that they were carrying bundles of cash.

Juan Rivera and Marvin Arguero kidnapped the two victims after they left a small back-alley Chinese restaurant. They took the couple to the marijuana farm, and locked them up in bamboo cages. Masako and Sung had already been murdered and buried.

Sami and Lu knew very little English. Rivera and Marvin beat the man about the head to find out about the money. The defendants had no Chinese verbal skills. The defendants found about ten thousand in Sami's purse and Lu's wallet. There were no money or valuables in their rental car. Even if he had wanted to reveal the whereabouts of the money, Lu couldn't communicate. They stripped Sami naked, and Cruz and Taigeras raped her in front of her husband.

The defendants became frustrated, and decided to ransack the couple's hotel room. They found the key for their Fiesta Hotel room in Sami's purse, and Rivera and Sumang left for a search. Another fifteen thousand was found, leaving about twenty-five thousand dollars still missing. If the defendants had been able to communicate, they would have known that Lu had placed a down payment on the small restaurant where they had dinner.

Sumang yelled louder and louder at the man, somehow believing that communication would improve with volume. Of course it didn't, and in a fit of rage, Sumang pulled out his military survival knife, and stabbed Lu through the heart four times. Lu died instantly and Sami began a long mournful scream. Rivera slapped her down, and gagged her with his filthy bandana. Gerardo took his duct tape from his truck and bound her arms and legs.

Rivera slapped his arm and said, "Don't bind her legs, asshole. How can we fuck her with his legs closed."

The defendants violated her repeatedly, including anal penetration. After the sixth attack, Sami went limp and died. The gag has suffocated her, as she had fought to get away from her attackers. Arguero and Cura took their turns fucking her, even

Continuin' On

after her body had cooled off.

Sami and Lu were identified by family DNA profiles. When Rivera had been arrested, he was still carrying Lu's wallet with about five thousand in cash. During Sumang's apprehension, a military survival knife was found in his truck and saved for evidence. Lab testing revealed Lu's blood deep inside the creases of the knife next to the handle.

With the exception of Sami and Lu, all the victims had been killed by hard blows with a blunt instrument to the back of their heads. Hair strands matching the victims were found on the clubs in the marijuana shed, and one of the bloody fingerprints on the smooth club had been identified as belonging to Jose Sumang.

The prosecutors from the Attorney General's Office (AGO) prepared the case for court trial. The motions for discovery and more time for defense preparation went on and on. The prosecutors found themselves dealing with eight different defense attorneys, one for each defendant. Every time a trail date was set, there would be a conflict with the private attorney's schedule, or sometimes, the defendant would want a change of attorney. During this whole fiasco, the CNMI was footing the bill for the prosecutors and the defense attorneys. This court delay went on for over a year. It became more nightmarish when the prosecutors asked to review the physical evidence, and much of it couldn't be found in the Police Property Room. The Property Custodian was related to two of the defendants.

As the year passed, the two originally assigned veteran prosecutors went onto other legal opportunities on the mainland, and the case got juggled back and forth between onboard prosecutors. Finally it landed in the lap of Bo Edwards and Nina Rosario.

Nina was fresh out law school and had just passed the CNMI

bar exam. She was enthused and excited about doing a major homicide case as her first felony prosecution. The truth was that she had not yet taken a misdemeanor case to court. But she was bright and knew the law.

Bo was another matter. He had drifted into Saipan after some questionable decisions dealing with escrow monies from his private law firm in South Carolina. He found the Saipan AGO about the time that they had no lawyers and they were desperate for legal help. So he was hired with a minimal background check. No one of record had ever seen him in a courtroom.

Bo was extremely obese and could barely walk. He was grouchy and had no friends. By the time the homicide case came along, Bo had never finished a case in criminal or civil court for the CNMI, and had never completed a project. He just blended into the woodwork except when he would piss someone off with his stupid remarks.

Fortunately for the prosecution of the case, the previous prosecutors had kept a thorough progress report. Without reading it, and especially without being updated on what needed to be done, Bo passed it to Nina, and asked her to do a synopsis.

He then waddled down to the nearby café for his morning snacks. He would probably bullshit for an hour or two, and then take an early, lengthy lunch. It was Friday, and probably didn't make much sense to return to the office.

Bo wasn't concerned about justice for Dina... or Eva, Masako, Sung, Sami or Lu. But he was interested in the pastas on special.

26

JILL FINDS LOVE AND COMMITMENT

Jill Flannigan and the tennis coach, Jonah, had been an item for over four months. Jill had been recovering from losing her husband, Mike, overboard during a storm in Palau. He had been lost at sea a year ago, and endless searches resulted in no sign of him. During his watch, he had neglected to strap himself in, and a giant wave washed him over the side and almost knocked down their 40-foot sailboat, the Waimea Star. Jill managed to sail the boat solo into the Palau harbor. Foul play was never suspected, as investigation showed that Jill and Mike had a sound marriage, and there was no large insurance policy. Weather recordings showed that there had been a large squall in their sailing quadrants.

Carlos and I had been in Palau on an embezzlement case. We met Jill, and invited her up to the hotel for some rest and relaxation. After selling her boat to a Hong Kong businessman, she showed up several weeks later, and started her recuperation from the grieving process. Her recovery program started with tennis and soon moved to Jonah who helped her re-enter the world of being alive and well. She knew that Jonah was a carefree soul, and would be her transition man. No one lied about the arrangement.

There are usually three-to-five pre-positioning supply ships anchored in the Saipan waters. These ships are loaded with military supplies and munitions, and are intended to sail anywhere in the Pacific Region on short notice. The ships are manned by merchant marine civilian types, many of whom are retired navy personnel. As old salts get close to the final retirement, they start thinking about leaving the sea, and settling down in a comfortable house with a garden and a white picket fence, and solid ground. This is exactly what happened with First Mate Steve Thompson.

Steve had heard through his sailing buddies that George and Jo could help him find a good wife through their match-maker business at the hotel. Two of his friends had found wonderful, loving Chinese wives, and had moved to the mainland. As fate would have it, Jill and Steve both ended up at the "fast date" round-robin session on the same night at the dating service. They were endlessly chatting away when George blew the time whistle and Steve had to move on to the next table.

When Jo compiled the dating interest notes late that evening, it was obvious that Jill wanted to see Steve again, and vice-versa. Jill had also listed two other men of interest, both Americans; and Steve had listed three other ladies, two Chinese and one Filipina. For the next two days, all the parties had a series of dates and dinners, with Jill moving Steve to her number one choice, but Steve listed Jill and a Chinese lady, Kina as a tie. Another several

Continuin' On

days of dating followed. Jill moved into the number one spot, and Jill and Steve ramped up their relationship to one on one.

Steve had to return to his ship for two weeks, but they stayed in touch by telephone and email, almost hourly. When Jonah heard the news, he volunteered to move back to his own place, and took his tooth brush and all his tennis gear. He handled it well, already having his eye on Kina. He offered to give Steve several free tennis lessons. Jill and the hotel maintenance crew spruced up her apartment, and moved in a new bed and fresh-smelling towels and sheets. Romance was clicking away in Jill's brain, and probably every tissue of her body.

When Steve came ashore, he checked into his regular dingy hotel. He had an old rust-bucket, miniature car called a Tiko, which he shared with his buddy who had just reported back to the ship for his two weeks of duty.

Steve and Jill met for dinner, and shared a few bottles of Chile wine. As with all new couples, they talked about families and future plans, and likes and dislikes. Much to Jill's delight, they were compatible. He had two grown children with several grandchildren, all living in the Western US. Jill had no children, and only an aging mother, and a long-lost brother. She was willing to live anywhere, as long as there were large bodies of water for sailing, even if it meant downsizing to a fourteen-foot dinghy.

Steve asked pointblank, "Where do we go from here? We're not teenagers. I really like you, bordering on love."

She said, "I was wondering how to say the same thing. I don't want you to think I'm some kind of hussy, some wild woman. I really like you too. Everything about you."

"Shall we move it to the next level?"

"I already did, last night in my dreams. You're one fine lover."

He said, "Let's find out for sure. You wanna wait another night, and think about it, or should I make my clumsy move right now and ask to be invited to your apartment?"

"Nope. I'll do the inviting. It's my apartment. Let's go, Sailor-boy."

They walked topside to her apartment, and looked out over the balcony and the full moon on the silver sea. They had their first real kiss, and off came the clothes. The rest of the night was loving and showering, followed by more loving and showering. Steve said, "Your body is so strong and athletic. You are one frisky female."

"Not having babies and lots of tennis will do that for a girl."

Steve said, "One more time? Or wait 'til morning?"

She said, "Let's snuggle." Peaceful sleep came in seconds.

As the sun came up, it was more loving and sweetness. For whatever reason, Jill felt that she had to tell him about Jonah. She said, "It's all over. It wasn't love. I just don't want people gossiping behind your back or you worrying that it might start up again."

He said, "Jill, we're going into this new and fresh. Your past is your past, as mine is also. Being an old saltwater sailor, I haven't been exactly pure my whole life. But that's behind me now. I want just you."

"Is that an offer of regular sex, or are we talking long-term commitment?"

"I'm talking marriage. Are you for it? I'm ready to put you on my insurance policies and checking account. I can retire anytime."

"That's the best wedding proposal I've heard all day. Shall we talk to George and Jo, and reserve the wedding chapel?"

Continuin' On

He said, "Let's do it. It's fast, only a month, but we're ready."

George set the date for them on Saturday at noon, and made all the arrangements for the license and the ceremony. Beachologist Fred took care of all the music, and ukuleles of course. I told him that his group should start charging a nominal fee. He laughed and said, "As long as we get one of Guangman's feasts, the jamming is well worth it. And besides we always need our practice sessions."

Steve and Jill wrote their own vows. I was the best man, and Cocina was the maid of honor. She was beautiful as ever, but dressed down a bit, not to out-shine the bride. But when we saw Jill, there was no out-shining this bride in her bright blue dress. She was glowing and gorgeous, and radiated happiness. Lola and Masako had covered her with orchids, plumerias and jasmine. She not only looked exquisite, but smelled like a walking flower shop.

As long as I'm mentioning attire, I should define the standard clothing worn by the groom and best man. That's what's so wonderful about the tropics. We had our usual walking shorts, bright aloha shirts, and *tsenalas*. It would be the same clothing for the beach feast and dancing under the stars.

After the ceremony and the music and dancing, Cocina had arranged for Steve and Jill to take out one of our power boats for a personal bay cruise. Jill had told Cocina that it's wonderful to make love out on the ocean under the wide-open sky. Cocina and I had experienced those sensations while sailing with our Aussie friends. Cocina placed padding and blankets on the boat, with an ice bucket of beer and champagne. Jill had lived on the ocean, so she would surely recognize Cocina's special preps.

The wedding party gave them a big send-off at the beach. And they literally sailed off into the red sunset, just like the movies.

The power boat had lights for night running. We watched them until they reached the horizon.

Suddenly three shots in quick succession rang out from the direction of the boat. Then it was quiet. I called the Police Rescue boat office. It took them over an hour to get to the hotel from the water side. I explained that Steve and Jill had taken off in a hotel boat, and then we heard the three shots. Steve and Jill hadn't come back. We heard no more shots.

Cocina's cell phone rang. It was Jill. She said that a large freighter almost ran them over as they were bobbing on the surface with the motor off. They saw a regular speed boat, maybe about sixteen feet, being lowered from the larger, mother ship. They decided it was time to get dressed and make a dash for shore. They thought it was a ship unloading narcotics or contraband to get around customs, or maybe smuggling people ashore.

Steve cranked up the motor and headed for the hotel. Apparently the engine noise alerted the freighter crew, and one of the crew started shining a large spotlight in a circle. The light found them, followed by three-four quick gun shots. Steve knew enough to avoid the bullets by running a zigzag pattern, and headed for one of the nearby pre-positioning ships. It was his ship, the Betty Louise. He got to the lee side of the ship, out of the gunfire range. The crew members heard him coming, and lowered their ropes, and brought their boat and them aboard. The captain reported the situation to the US Coast Guard.

After everyone calmed down, Captain Felix Carter of the Betty Louise congratulated the couple on their wedding and allowed them to stay aboard until daybreak. Jill got to check out Steve's cabin, and was happy to see that Steve was not a stereotype sailor, with pin-ups on the wall, or photos of all his ex-girlfriends. His

Continuin' On

room was neat and orderly. There was no time for love-making, and sleep was impossible, as Steve's buddies kept dropping by to get a peep at the bride.

Steve and Jill were uninjured. There were no bullet holes in their boat. Steve surmised that the shots were only intended to scare them away.

Later, the Coast Guard and Police Boat Patrol made several runs in the area of the freighter. It was gone. There was no aerial surveillance available. They completed another search at daybreak with the same results.

A jogger found a speedboat roped to a mangrove tree about ten o'clock. No operator was to be found. The boat had no numbers or papers, or any way of identifying ownership or country of origin. There was Chinese writing on the inboard motor, which turned out to be a well-known manufacturer.

The local man who owned the land claimed salvage rights if the operator wasn't found. The Coast Guard did the paperwork, and took the boat into harbor for possible evidence and investigation. The captain said that the landowner would get the boat if no one stepped forward to claim it.

Steve moved in with Jill. She offered to drive him to the dock when it was time to go back to his ship for duty. Divine intervention struck the island. The Tiko died on the road the next day, and Steve signed it over to the first senior citizen that came walking by. The senior said that he had never owned a car before, and rebuilding the car would be a good project for his old age. His government identification card from *manamko* showed that he was already eight-two years old. It's good to have ambitions and goals.

The whole shooting and boating incident was forgotten until a few days later. Then the assassinations began.

27

FIVE DOWN – THREE TO GO

There are thousands of Chinese people walking around Saipan in the evening. Most of them are garment workers who have finished work for the day, and are out socializing and enjoying their friends, and staying cool after working in the factories all day. As with any ethnic group, most are law-abiding good citizens. Others are prostitutes, gamblers, thieves, and some sell drugs. Very few are assassins.

When Chow Li and Ling Lo left their boat in the mangrove swamp, it was simply a matter of contacting their island associates and blending in with thousands of other Chinese. They already had island cell phones and the numbers to call. They weren't worried about being picked out as outsiders. The locals liked to say, "There are no ways of telling the Chinese apart. They all look the same." That would work for their mission.

Chow and Ling were not ordinary Chinese males. They were both rubber stamps of Bruce Lee. They moved like panthers on their tip of their toes. The local Chinese knew who they were

Continuin' On

and showed them proper respect, never looking them fully in the eyes. Most Chinese knew the tattoo symbols. They were members of the powerful Shining Dragon Tong, sent by the Tong boss, Mr. Hyun Woo, to avenge the murder of his god-daughter and her husband in the mountain marijuana fields. Woo had assigned two of his best men, both professional and tight-lipped, and with a long successful record of taking care of business.

Their contacts told them that seven of the assailants had been released on bail. The families had put up all their houses and land holdings as collateral to ensure their return to court. The local justices kept the bail low, knowing that the chances of conviction were unlikely. The victims were all outsiders, and the jury would be composed of local people, many of whom would be related to the defendants. The commissioner kept Ricardo Zambales in custody for his own safety. Ricardo was more than willing to stay put, and was trading his testimony for freedom. He hoped to get away to the mainland, maybe blend into the millions of people in New York.

The Chinese translators in court knew the movements of the defendants. The sleaze-balls had to check in with the court periodically, and some of the translators knew the defendants personally. Chow and Ling were told that the ringleader, Juan Rivera, liked to drink beer and smoke grass with Jose Sumang and Geraldo Cura, at Pau Pau Beach. Sometimes the defendants stayed at the beach all night and became completely and stumbling drunk. They would be defenseless against any attack.

Chow and Ling checked out the beach every night for the three defendants. On the fourth night, three defendants showed up, along with another defendant, Jack Fernandez. They knew it was Jack by the photographs furnished by the translators. Chow and Ling were watching from the heavy brush. The defendants had brought along a local girl, Joyce Ann, who was busily servicing all four men. Several hours later, everyone settled down in front of a fire. The men were wasted, and lost interest in the girl. After a quick bath in the ocean, she was soon fast asleep in the back of a pick-up truck.

The mosquitoes were out in full force. Most men would have been agitated and half-crazy sitting in the brush being attacked by the bugs. Chow and Ling sat quietly. They had brought along protective clothing and were wearing insect repellant. They had managed to find dog treats for the boonie dogs if they happened to wander by, foraging for garbage.

By four AM, the four defendants were fast asleep in a row on the sand. Chow and Ling checked their 9mm semi-autos with full silencers. They listened for any sound and watched for any distraction, and moved out confidently. Each man had already picked out his two targets.

Two quick shots to each head, and it was over in seconds. Chow looked over at Ling, and nodded towards the girl in the truck. She was apparently still asleep. Ling gave him a "thumbs down" sign, and Chow shot her three times in the chest. Her eyes never opened. Gone to the long sleep.

The assassins weren't concerned about footprints. They were wearing new, non-descript tsenalas, like thousands of others on Saipan. The cartridges left in the scene would not be an issue, as there wouldn't be any weapons for a match-up. They returned to the brush, and made certain that they had left no evidence. They were not smokers and did not eat or drink while hiding.

The walked back through the brush and left in their white sedan, rented to a fictitious Filipino should it ever be identified.

Continuin' On

They drove out to Banzai Cliff, dismantled their pistols, and threw the parts into the ocean over a wide area. The water is hundreds of meters deep in this section, and it was likely that the metal parts would rust out before they ever washed ashore. They threw away their tsenalas on different parts of the road, and took their new ones from a paper bag. Fingerprints would be impossible on the rough rubber surfaces. They wadded up the paper bag, and threw it in a murky water swamp area.

The assassins returned to their lodgings, and slept until noon. They were awakened by two beautiful young Chinese ladies who prepared their breakfast. Love making followed, and a long, leisurely nap. About four PM, the men were nudged awake by the ladies. Chow and Ling swapped ladies and made love again. The ladies refused money, giggled, and promptly left. Moments later, an elderly man entered, carrying their new weapons and a schedule of activities of the remaining four defendants.

The elderly Chinese man gave Chow and Ling a description of the crime scene where the defendants and their woman had been assassinated. He had watched from the top of a hill at the confusion. He said the responding officers contaminated the crime scene within minutes, walking over the footprints, and in some cases, actually burying the cartridge cases in the sand with their heavy feet. To take advantage of the shade, the police and media had stupidly parked in the brush area where the assassins had been hiding,

The commissioner arrived and berated several of the officers for their incompetence. The investigation then took some form of order, but it was too late. The assassins had no worries about being discovered through the amateurish crime scene investigators.

The four remaining defendants were going to be tougher to eliminate. Two of them, Arturo Taigeras and Marvin Arguero, had immediately asked for sanctuary in the jail, while Ricardo Zambales was still in protective custody. Leonardo Cruz was still on the outside. He told Arturo, "I'm not afraid of anybody."

The elderly man gave Chow and Ling the address for Leonardo, and where he liked to drink and play poker in San Antonio. The man bowed and left.

Chow and Ling talked and planned. They decided to let everything quiet down, and then take out Cruz. They waited several days, and picked up another rental car. Chow knew the slain god-daughter from his school days. He had wanted to marry the girl, but her parents though him unworthy. Assassins do not make the most desirable husbands. Ling reminded him not to make her murder a personal matter. Chow nodded, but calmly decided to eliminate Cruz in a close-up manner, using a stiletto. He wanted to see his eyes as he faded away.

Chow and Ling surveilled the Lucky Boy poker arcade for several nights. They were in the midst of hundreds of Chinese workers, and hardly stood out. Cruz followed a basic pattern of coming from home about eight o'clock and going inside the poker arcade. Chow and Ling stood next to him on several nights, watching his moves and attitude. He wasn't reluctant about pushing someone off a poker machine where he wanted to play. He was loud and obnoxious, especially to the female Chinese poker attendants.

On the third night of surveillance, Chow decided it was time. He waited for him inside the exit veranda. As Cruz left about midnight, Ling got his attention by calling out his name.

Cruz said, "Hey asshole, how do you know my name?" Those

Continuin' On

were his last words.

Chow moved in behind him, and threw an arm bar hold around his neck. He slid his stiletto through his left side, piercing Cruz's heart. Chow twisted the knife several times for good order, and said something in Chinese to the effect of "go to hell motherfucker." Chow and Ling took the body and set it up on a veranda couch. Because he died instantly, there wasn't much blood. They covered the front of the victim with a rug. Cruz appeared to be taking a nap.

When they turned to leave, they saw a middle-aged Chinaman watching them. He was wide-eyed and obviously frightened. They had seen him playing poker earlier.

Chow knew that he would have enough sense not to cross the Tong. They told him in Chinese "to be blind and forgetting." He nodded affirmatively and mumbled an agreement. Chow got his local address, and the address of his family in Canton. Ling made a slicing movement across his throat, and the man nodded even faster.

Chow and Ling walked casually from the poker arcade. Five down, and three to go. Chow had enjoyed the killing. He had read the crime reports smuggled out by the Chinese translators. He felt joyful in avenging his friend's murder.

They talked to one of Hyun Woo's lieutenants through an encrypted Chinese cellular phone. The lieutenant agreed that they could come home until the trials began. Woo was happy with their progress report. He was arranging for the bodies of his god-daughter and her husband to be cremated, and the ashes flown home to China. Ling gave their new weapons back to the elderly Chinese man for use on the next mission.

A non-marked twenty-foot vessel showed up two nights later,

during a new moon phase. Chow and Ling were soon gone into the night. Within two hours, they were back on the mother ship, enjoying a relaxing ocean cruise on the way back to China. The trial would begin in about two months. There would be plenty of time for earned fine cuisine and aged wine, and gorgeous women at the karaoke bar.

28

THE USELESS FAT PROSECUTOR

The trial date was set. It was definite for August, and the judge emphatically said from the bench, "There will no more delays. You lawyers need to get everything squared away. No more feeble excuses. Cancel any outside plans for that month." He assigned two defense lawyers per defendant, just to offset the chance that one became sick, one moved onto another job, or just became frightened about being around the violent defendants and their dysfunctional families.

There were only three defendants left—Ricardo Zambales, Arturo Taigeras and Marvin Arguero. Because of his informant status, Zambales had two armed corrections officers assigned to him at all times, including the courtroom and in the jail.

The police had screwed up the murder investigations of the other defendants. The inept investigators had never experienced multiple murders of such a magnitude. There were no leads or workable information. They decided the murders had been committed over the affections of the local girl Joyce Ann, probably from one of her many male acquaintances. The FBI declined to work with the local bozos on the murder case. Their reputation had been taking a lot of hits since the 9/11 tragedies, and the director wanted only good news, not another failed case way out in the tropics.

Fernando Cruz's death had been written off as a poker dispute. The Chinaman who had witnessed the murder remained mute, and opted to quit his Saipan sewing job and return to his family in China. The Crime Stopper's group put out messages to the community offering a reward for information about the murders. It never crossed the mind of the program coordinator to place the request on the Chinese or Filipino radio and television stations. All the posted flyers on the bulletin boards and telephone poles were in English.

The local families came to our Investigations Agency as a group, and asked for help in the investigations. They were respectful and pleading for help. They never realized that I was Dina's brother-in-law, and that Carlos was our family's best friend. Most of them never considered the victims in the case, but only thought of the defendants. Just like society often does. They garnered my polite response, that they "should let the police handle it. We are overwhelmed with cases, too many to count."

After they left, Carlos said, "Fuck them. They knew what kind of asshole kids they raised. Some of the parents were in and out jails for years."

I said, "Let's do something clean and fun. Get out the sail boards." We played in the water until sunset.

Chow and Ling were told that the trial was starting, and that they should return to Saipan to eliminate the remaining three. Woo was happy with their work and gave them a hefty bonus for their families. It was not spoken out loud, but it was likely that

Continuin' On

there would be sacrifices and losses incurred if they had to get close to the defendants. Chow and Ling put all their personal affairs in order before they left.

Chow and Ling accepted the danger, and reluctantly pulled themselves from the warm, lusty beds of their mistresses. The men has been sharing four women provided by Woo. As the assassins left on their mission, all four women sat stoically, now uncertain about their futures and where Woo would send them next. He would not want them at his home. Woo liked only young virgin girls from the country. The more innocent, the better.

Chow and Ling had no thoughts about the women. They focused on the assassinations, and their Saipan contacts. This time they were going in as tourists. The China routes to Saipan had recently opened up to Chinese visitors. They flew to Saipan first class, throwing down umbrella drinks and enjoying steak dinners.

Bo and Nina studied the prosecution notes and prepared for trial. Once again, the evidence was reviewed, and again, much of it had disappeared. The FBI laboratory had experienced "the missing evidence" problem before in the CNMI, and they had carefully prepared duplicate reports as feasible. Bo hadn't met with his key witness, Zambales, and had left this necessary chore to Nina. Zambales began to get fuzzy on his recollections, and it was obvious that he had decided it would be better to go to prison, then be loose on the streets waiting for the assassins. Being an island boy, Zambales had no idea that there were hit men in prisons. He had never heard of the White Aryan Brotherhood, the Mexican Mafia, or the Crips. He only knew about secret tongs through Jet Li movies.

Jury selection was a farce. Bo didn't object to certain people, even through his local jury advisor had doubts about the objectivity of certain candidates for the panel. He didn't appear overly concerned about some of the family connections. At one stage, the judge asked Bo if he felt a second cousin to Defendant Arguero could be fair and objective. Bo replied, "Yes, your honor. I think the female cousin will look at only the facts." Bo allowed several candidates with minor criminal backgrounds to be empanelled.

On each *voir dire*, the judge shook his head and said, "Continue." He cautioned Bo several more times. The defense counsels just looked down and sniggered. Counsel Laurie Hershberg said to her colleague Jerry Boyd, "Slam-dunk. The boys are going to walk." Nina looked down and away, embarrassed even before the actual trial was underway.

The jury was finally selected after a long, dreary day. It was painful to watch. To keep the trial moving, the defense only objected to two potential jurors, one former policeman and a retired executive from the mainland. Bo helped the defense in most of his selections.

Chow and Ling were on-island, and quietly tucked away in their former hidden apartment. Their contacts had provided them with three Glock 9mm pistols, two grenades, and a long-distance Remington sniper rife with a scope, which folded nicely into a briefcase. The rifle was a newer M-24 bolt-action model, refitted in New Rockford, North Dakota, with a Leopold and Stevens scope MKIV/M3A. It fired an effective 7.62 NATO round. Chow had trained with the same model of rifle before in his spy programs in China. His American practice weapon had been stolen and smuggled out of Iraq.

All the armaments had been clandestinely purchased from part-time soldiers at the Guam armory through third and fourth parties.

Continuin' On

There was no way of tracing the weapons back to Chow and Ling. Over the next few days, they watched the trial operation from a distance, and especially how the three defendants were transported to the court from the nearby jail, and into the courtroom. They dressed like ordinary garment manufacturing workers.

Bo's opening statements about the guilt of the three defendants had been written out by Nina. It made sense and summarized what the prosecution would prove. She outlined the evidence and circumstances and how it tied together with Zambales upcoming testimony. But Bo's delivery was substandard and puerile. Either he hadn't read the opening statement, or he was a nervous fool, or both. His delivery prompted the judge to ask, "Prosecutor, do you need time to prepare your opening statement? You seem unfamiliar with the information." Nina looked away.

He answered, "Yes your honor. Maybe we could break for lunch?"

The judge, replied, "Counsel, it's only 10AM. Let's keep moving."

Bo continued on. He stuttered and sweated, and asked if he could sit for his statement. He was breathing heavily and obviously hyperventilating. Now, even the defense counsels were embarrassed about someone in their profession being so fucking incompetent and useless.

The judge asked, "Do you need the paramedics?"

Bo replied, "No, I'm okay. But maybe we could break for lunch?" He was gasping for sources of fresh oxygen.

The judge agreed and said, "Counsel, get yourself set-up with a chair and microphone for the afternoon session. Read your notes and make a professional delivery."

The judge looked over at Nina and said, "Get him up to speed, or make the opening presentation yourself."

Nina stood up and answered, "Yes, your honor. We'll get it together." Nina helped Bo walk out of the courtroom. He kept puffing for air.

Chow and Ling had developed a plan to take out at least two of the defendants. Zambales was brought over separately from another part of the jail with two police officers. They would get him later. Taigeras and Arguero were brought over chained together with their feet shackled, usually with two corrections guards. They couldn't run out of range. All three defendants wore bright orange jumpsuits. Easy targets.

There was a three-story telephone company building that looked out over the exit door at the jail, about one hundred and forty meters away. There would be plenty of time to get away after the shots. An attached ladder was at the rear of the building. The red flame trees were in full bloom, and covered the ladder from the view of nearby pedestrians. Chow parked his non-descript rental car in back of the building and scurried up the ladder. He was carrying a briefcase. It was daytime and there would be little distinctive muzzle flash from the rifle.

The plan was basic and direct. Chow had learned the American KISS acronym in his Chinese spy training—*Keep It Simple Stupid*. It was especially plausible with the local inadequate cops and the minimal response from the federal agents. The feds were undermanned, and totally immersed in several high profile drug and money laundering cases.

Ling was in front of the nearby police station and near the library. Chow watched for Taigeras and Arguero to exit the jail. They did, right on schedule, not wearing bullet-resistant vests. He

Continuin' On

let Ling know by cell phone. Within a fraction of a second, with a five-second time delay on the grenades, Ling pulled the pins, and lobbed one under a police car, and threw the second near a car at the library. No innocent persons were nearby to be injured. He hid behind a huge ironwood tree as the grenades ignited.

The police car had recently been topped off. The grenade set off over twenty gallons of fuel from the tank, and the fumes and liquid exploded high over the parking lot. It was a spectacular explosion and fire ball.

Before the grenades exploded, Chow had already selected Taigeras as his first target, an easy shot at the one hundred and forty-meter range. The weather was perfect, just a few clouds moving overhead. He fired two quick shots, hitting Taigeras full in the chest. When the grenades went off as the major diversion, Arguero stopped full in his tracks, and provided a standing still shot for Chow. Three rapid shots to his head and chest dropped Arguero to the asphalt driveway. The officers couldn't figure out where the shots came from. They ducked for cover, believing they might be the next targets. With their standard .38 caliber revolvers, they were ill-equipped to counter a sniper rifle. The two explosions and emergency responses added to the commotion and confusion.

Chow packed up his rifle and stepped down the back ladder. He was careful to take the empty cartridge casings with him. He didn't see anyone watching him, but saw dozens of people running towards the explosions. His rental car started up, and he drove away through the back of the island as he heard sirens coming from all directions. Ling slowly walked over to the beach from the police parking lot, picked up his counterfeit Birkenstock sandals, a colorful Hawaii beach towel, and his Prada beach bag from the sand, and walked south along the sea to his lodgings in San Antonio.

Both Taigeras and Arguero were pronounced dead at the scene by responding paramedics. It started to rain. Much of any remaining evidence was washed away at the scene of the two explosions and from the rooftop of the telephone building. No credible witnesses had come forward. There was a great deal of controversy as to whether rifle shots had been heard, and whether there were there more than the two grenade explosions. One Palauan woman thought that she saw a Chinese man with a paper bag in the parking lot, but couldn't identify the man except to say, "He looked like a Chinese guy. I think he was wearing cheap flip-flops."

Carlos and I watched the investigation from the roof of the Beach Hotel. I said, "Whatsa think? Any arrests anytime soon?" The television crews were already doing live coverage.

He replied, "Those killers are pros. They know the game. One of them likely used the roof of the telephone building for their sniper shots. Think the bozos will figure that out?"

I said, "Highly unlikely they'll sort that out. Let's get out of the rain. Feel like a shot or two of Mexican tequila?"

Carlos answered, "I be ready. Those killers probably have gold-embossed business cards from China that read, *We Deliver Justice*. I'm betting that someone back home got real pissed off about one of the Chinese murder victims."

"Yep, the assholes delivered justice. Sometimes that's the only way." Vigilante justice can be rash and unpredictable, but it is effective. If you got the right person every time.

The court closed down until the following week. The security was doubled on the last defendant, Zambales. During the week,

Continuin' On

the judge met with the attorney general and Bo was quietly reassigned back to civil suits against the government involving potholes on the roadway, personnel matters involving tardiness, and illegal tree cutting. In the privacy of his chambers, the judge asked the attorney where he had found such "a fat-fuck, dipshit, waste-of-skin asshole." The attorney general said that Bo had slipped between the cracks with three previous attorney generals, but he promised to evaluate Bo further, and get him re-trained or fired. The attorney general admitted that he had never observed Bo in court.

Nina showed promise in the review of the case, and was left to assist a new veteran prosecutor. She sighed with relief when she heard the news, thinking that probably her career was in the crapper before it ever got started.

Zambales' attorney, Mack Davis, made contact with Nina, and said that Zambales wanted to make a deal, and get off the island before he was killed. Nina and the new AGO prosecutor Mike Robles met with Davis, and the deal was struck. Because of his cooperation in the case, Zambales would not get life imprisonment but a twenty-year sentence and incarceration in a federal prison on the mainland. The judge upped the sentence to twenty-five years with no possibility of parole. Zambales went for it, and agreed to the conditions in open court. He wanted out of Saipan as soon as possible.

Next day, Zambales was flown to the supermax Federal Prison known as ADX Florence near Pueblo, Colorado. He would count as his new acquaintances notorious figures such Theodore Kaczynski, Terry Nichols, Richard Reid and Zacarias Moussaoui. He would be let out of his solitary cell one hour a day for showers and exercise. His food would be served through an opening in his door, and he would be viewed constantly on a video surveillance camera. His raping and marijuana days were finished.

Chow and Ling stayed current with the case developments through the Chinese translators, and from the television and newspapers. Chow called home on his Chinese encrypted cellular phone, and they were instructed to enjoy their holiday for another two weeks, and then return home on the regular flight. Woo asked the assassins to bring him and his two new teenager girls several Saipan T-shirts, some sparkly face tattoos, and six bags of coconut candy.

Chow and Ling, and their Chinese island contact went fishing in a private rented boat. Once past the reef, Chow dismantled the sniper rifle and handguns, and dropped the parts over the side as they trolled for tuna in one hundred meter deep waters. The rifle briefcase also went over the side filled with rocks. The trip paid off with the catch of two forty-pound yellow fin tunas. The world's best sashimi would be on the evening menu.

Woo called Chow and said that Zambales would be eliminated later in another way. Zambales wasn't going anywhere, and would not be forgotten. Woo had significant influence with the handlers of the Asian prisoners currently in the federal prison system. Most of them were relatives or brothers in the tong, and owed him favors and special loans.

Chow and Ling's former mistresses had been re-assigned to two new German lawyers setting up in China. Woo said that the assassins would be happy with their new ladies, whom he had personally selected and trained.

29

TANO ANTIGO v. MABUHAY POWER

During the recent slowdown down in the CNMI economy, a ragtag, uneducated group of local islanders *Tano Antigo* organized themselves into an anti-alien worker association. Most of them were unemployed and were able to stage public demonstrations during regular work hours. There was no problem getting off work. They didn't work. But they carried placards with vitriolic messages such as "Go home. This is Our Land" and "No Way. Stay Off Our Island." They knew they had the rights of free speech and assembly but had no idea where the authority came from.

Some of the local motorists passing by the demonstrations honked their horns, and flashed the "thumps up" sign. This just stimulated the demonstrators and caused them to stay longer, and get more vocal.

One of my Filipino-American friends summed it up, and said "Assholes. They have no idea who builds their roads and bridges, or teaches their children in school, or provides medical care for their babies and aging parents. They couldn't discuss what the US Constitution means. They didn't work and study for their citizenship like I did. It was just given to them on a silver platter."

During the rest of the time, the demonstrators burned up their day drinking under coconut trees and grousing about the foreigners. They wanted to have the managerial and professional positions that were held mostly by educated, trained foreign workers from the P.I., Korea, China and Japan. The majority of the demonstrators wouldn't know where to turn a computer on, and most couldn't name one of the programs.

The ragtag group didn't want the jobs working in the hot sun in construction, farming and grounds maintenance earning a minimum wage. Because they traced their ancestry back hundred of years, overlooking their intermixing with Carolinians, Spanish, Filipino, Chinese and Japanese, somehow they believed they were entitled to the high paying positions without training, apprenticeships, and education, and paying their dues like you do in any occupation. They wanted everything handed to them just like the United States granted them their US citizenship in 1986, just with the signature by the President. They liked to badmouth the US but were first in line for federal grants, work programs, food stamps, typhoon relief, and subsidized housing.

The mainland Americans and foreign workers provided the medical personnel, the engineers, the lawyers, the scientists and the teachers, because in most cases, local people had not prepared themselves by going to college. Many of the islanders wanted to maintain old traditions of fishing and farming, and had little concept of globalization, and that the whole world was a huge

Continuin' On

community of interaction and blending of ideas and manufacturing. They also had forgotten that farming and fishing are tough jobs.

I watched the group and recognized a dozen of them as troublemakers. I had seen one of the females in and out of my hotel, just needing a "hot bed" for a few hours. One of the fellows, Carlos and I had arrested for cattle rustling, and another was a well-known dope dealer. I asked Carlos, "They want to get rid of the Filipinos and return to the old ways, like farming and fishing? They don't look like they could bait a hook or plant a *kamote*."

He laughed and said, "They're good at video games and drinking beer. Look at their hands. There's not a hard worker in the group."

"I see some people in the mob that look exactly like Filipinos, and some that are halfa-halfas."

Carlos smiled, "Everybody here is a mixture of races and cultures. That's one of the great things about Saipan. Somehow or another, however, some of the youngsters got the idea that they were "pure" Chamorro. There hasn't been a pure Chamorro since the 1600's when the Marianas Islands became a Spanish colony. Ask some of the fools why they have names like Mendoza and Fleming, and Cing and Norita. Could it be from the Spanish and visitors to the island? They have no idea of their real history."

The riff-raff members were primarily vocal about a Filipino organization called *"Mabuhay Power,"* a group of Filipinos that was trying to improve its immigration status and become US citizens. Most of the Filipino group had been in the CNMI for over five years, and many had been long-time residents of up to thirty years. They bore their children on Saipan, had attended local schools, and many of their offspring were in the US Armed Forces. They had inter-married with indigenous peoples. In most categories, they were already Americans, except for the legal document. They were going through the legal channels, just as the Latin Americans had done in years past to gain legal immigration status in the US.

Carlos and I found ourselves pulled into the issue when the motley group began vandalizing Filipino and Chinese vehicles. We had a windshield broken in one of our employee's cars at the hotel. There were also some instances where foreign workers had been pushed and shoved at community events, and some had received threatening phone calls at their homes. Three of our Filipino hotel workers had been told "to leave the island" while they were shopping at the public market. One had actually been punched in the jaw.

Through Commissioner Lois Harding, Carlos inquired if he was still a deputized police officer with the police department. He told her that he was tired of these bigoted punks going around threatening hard working people. She confirmed that he was still deputized, and offered the help of her investigators.

Carlos said to me, "Let's start with an easy one. Myla, Aubrey and Mario were threatened with bodily injury at the market. Mario was sucker-punched when he tried to walk away. They know the assholes. Let's interview everyone, and go get an arrest warrant, and take their butts to jail." Carlos was on the trail and he was pissed.

I said, "Right on, my brother." The three were arrested the following week for the threats and disturbing the peace. I helped Carlos arrest two, and a village cop picked up the third.

I enjoyed watching Carlos work. His Chamorro lineage was

Continuin' On

interwoven with his Japanese ancestors, and he fit the stereotype of the methodical, relentless Asian worker. Once he had the mission, little could deter him long-term. On a temporary basis, I could often slow him from the track with a fresh baked donut, or a big juicy hamburger with extra onions and tomatoes. He always found time for junk food, and then went right back to work.

A middle-aged Chinese businessman came to our agency with a complaint that his aged mother had been hit by rock thrown at her house. He knew who the assailant was. Cocina walked into our office and heard most of the conversation. We promised to help. Now the stakes had moved up to the felony level, and we could make the arrest based on probable cause. The man provided us with the names of several witnesses, and he gave us the half-pound rock that had hit his mother, for evidence. He had called the police and after two hours, he figured out that they would never respond. His mother had been treated for a minor leg injury at the hospital and released.

Carlos told the man there would be no charge for our work. After he left, Cocina said, "You gonna catch the perp, and neck him out? Make him do the chicken?"

I glanced at Carlos and just shook my head. Carlos busted up. Cocina said, "What? Why are you guys giving me those looks?"

I said, "You've been watching those Hollywood cop movies again... right?"

"Yeah, and there's another one tomorrow." She was determined to learn the English language, movie-style. I loved her more every day.

"Yeah, baby. If he's really bad, we'll make him do the turkey."

She left the office with a look of bewilderment. Knowing her, she would be searching though her slang dictionary and asking her American friends about "doing the turkey."

The arrest of the felony assault suspect came off without a hitch, as it mostly does with punks. He was an opportunist from Chuuk, an outlying Micronesian island. He had decided to get in good with the local islanders by threatening and hitting an old lady with a rock. He wasn't aware that there was on-going legislation that would put his father out of work, and would allow only locals from the CNMI to hold jobs.

As fast as the ridiculous group began, its overt racism and discrimination messages came to a public halt. Their grandstanding was compared to the beginning of Nazi regime in Germany, and the hate propaganda vomited up from the KKK and the White Aryan Brotherhood. Some of the local politicians not only distanced themselves from the organization, but were vocal in their disapproval. They opposed confrontation and endorsed diplomacy. Two of the senators reminded the demonstrators that indigenous rights aren't upheld with hatred and warnings of violence. Another senator said, "They are a misguided group gone astray. Everything they do is reckless and counterproductive." This criticism from the politicians was especially noteworthy since it was an election year, and the locals were the ones who could vote, and not the foreign workers. Maybe democracy and fair play were taking root.

The strongest condemnation came from the bishop. He said that the racial messages were contrary to the teachings of Christ and were against God's wishes for love and harmony among people. He said the problems with vandalism, theft, hatred and domestic violence had to stop. He said that the people "should hold hands and work together" and not oppose one another. He added that the local people should be helping the other groups in

Continuin' On

their citizenship efforts. He reminded the Chamorro leaders that they and the Filipinos were united in the same church, and that many of the CNMI priests were from the Philippines. Catholics listen to their bishops.

Community elders took it upon themselves to inform the demonstrators that they needed to grow up, and accept the responsibilities of being positive and helpful islanders in the middle of the Pacific. They were also reminded that on Saipan, we are a rainbow of cultures, ethnicity, languages, and traditions. Diversity should be part of everyone's vocabulary and in practice, not just to be politically correct. Driving a wedge between different segments of society was intolerable. One of the traditional leaders said that the CNMI should be known for its vibrant culture, pristine and white sand beaches, tourist friendly people, gorgeous views, and many historical sites; and not for bigoted and nasty behavior.

Carlos said, "Yeah, they should do all that, but first, they need to get their sorry asses into a classroom. If they were studying, they wouldn't have time for all this other bullshit." I agreed. Adios to ignorance and prejudice.

Learning to live in peace and love is good, but I intended to watch the demonstrators and their motives. Rhetoric from both sides are only words. I wanted to see what their future actions would be. The racial garbage might still persist. Sometimes cockroaches go underground and only come out in darkness to do their destruction.

Biba Marianas.

30

THE THREE BROS

Sitting on my balcony one afternoon, I got a long distance call from my younger brother Zeke. His wife had died about a year ago after a long, courageous bout with cancer. She was a fighter. Zeke had literally gone fishing in Idaho and Alaska for about six months to get through the grieving process. When he got back to California, we stayed in touch over the phone and email. I had sent him brochures and stories from the islands, and he promised to make a visit. I told him at the time to bring our middle brother, Jed, with him, and we would charter a fishing boat, get a good guide, and do all fourteen islands in the CNMI.

He said, "Tommy boy, we are coming, Jed and I. We're coming!"

"How did you talk Jed into it? He's kinda of a homebody, and doesn't like traveling with all this terrorism bullcrap going on."

"I know, but his wife told him to go and take a break, that a trip would good for him, and their marriage. I think they've been married for over thirty years. He wouldn't know what

Continuin' On

another pussy looked like."

I answered, "Yeah, lots of pussy here. But I bet it was the fishing that got him searching for his favorite reels."

"Yep, the boy loves his fishing. He's fished all the Pacific waters from Mexico to Canada. Got some giants too."

"This is great. You'll get a chance to meet Cocina and the three kids. There's some great people out here. You will love it."

He said, "We're coming for a month. Got a room for us at the inn? And how about fishing gear?"

"Got your room, no problem. Just bring your favorite reels. Everything else is here. For clothes, you'll need some shorts and T-shirts, and maybe a pair of long pants. You can get durable straw hats here. Our shirt maker at the hotel, Kaylene, will make you aloha shirts that will be the envy of everyone back home."

He said his goodbyes. They would arrive in about two weeks. I told Cocina, and she got into "getting ready for the VIPS mode." I slowed her down, and said these characters were my brothers, and would be decked out in shorts and tank tops. Nothing fancy would be needed or expected.

Their marital situations interested her to no end. I could see that Zeke and Jed would not only be fishing and drinking margaritas on the beach, but would be busy with blind dates and the ladies.

Carlos and I picked them up at the airport. The bros looked happy and healthy and in good physical shape. Carlos had already arranged for a boat and guide Arnie Arizapa. He said that he would come along and knew people on two of the northern islands, Pagan and Anatahan, where we could stay and make camp.

Cocina loved the bros right away, and vice versa. After a few umbrella drinks, Guangman brought out a tropical feast par excellence.

He introduced the bros to sogu, his favorite drink from Korea.

After dinner, we built a fire in the pit at water's edge, and talked about the old times, not all good but mostly damn good times. Cocina didn't waste time introducing her matchmaking ideas.

She asked Zeke, "Have you got over the loss of your wife yet?" She was direct and pragmatic.

He answered, "Yeah mostly. Sometimes it's tough when the family gets together, and we talk about the children and our trips and the holidays. But I'm okay. My wife Marion expected me to go on with my life. She gave me a list of potential mates, but they didn't fit into my plans. They had stable jobs and families, and wanted to stay in California. I want to travel, and to fish and hunt, and maybe have a few crazy adventures in my so-called sunset years."

Cocina asked, "You want to meet some of my lady friends?"

Zeke asked, "Do they look like you?"

"A couple of them are much prettier. And they have jobs."

"Oh baby, bring them on down."

She looked at Jed and asked, "How about you, Jed? Are you almost a single man?"

He smiled and said, "I don't think so. We're still working on where we're at. Been married a long time."

I watched my little wife say, "Good for you. If you get ready, I can find you a friend, or maybe you just need someone to talk to."

Jed said, "That's a good idea. Maybe after our fishing trip up north."

Cocina nodded her head past the bar tables, and soon Marcella appeared. She's one of my favorite people, smart and a unbelievable sense of humor.

Cocina said, "Marcella, met Zeke. He's the brother that I was

Continuin' On

telling you about. And the other brother is Jed."

Marcella said hello, and sat down next to Zeke. Guangman brought us all fresh drinks, and we talked until the barkeep hit the bell for closing time. The bros said goodnight, and off they went to their third floor room. The jet lag would hit soon. Within a few days, they would be adjusted to the climate and the time differences between Saipan and the mainland.

Cocina couldn't contain herself and said to Marcella, words right off the afternoon television shows, "Well girlfriend. Does he cut it? Does he make the grade?"

Marcella said, "Oh, he's a good-looking one. Almost as cute as Tom Parker."

She added, "Nobody comes close to my Tommy."

I gave a little blush and said, "Thank you, ladies. It's true."

Cocina gave me a snappy punch on the shoulder.

Marcella said, "Zeke looks in good shape and healthy. But do you think he's going to be a playboy or settle down?"

I said, "Hey, you just met. You're not getting married tomorrow. But I can tell you he's not a lothario type. He and Marion lived in Las Vegas for about eight years, and they were never party-goers or gamblers."

She said, "How about Jed? He's cute too, but very quiet."

I said, "He's the middle brother. The middles ones are always watching and listening, but tend to be quiet and out of the family arguments. He hasn't figured out his marriage situation yet."

She looked at Cocina and asked, "Do you think Zeke will call me?"

"No doubt, but probably not for a week or so. The bros are going fishing."

Zeke and Jed joined us for breakfast the next morning. Zeke

asked Cocina for her cell phone and Marcella's number. He walked out on the beach and made his call. He seemed to forget about breakfast.

Cocina just kept smiling. She's so smug and righteous when her matchmaking takes hold.

Jed said, "Good for him. He's back among the living."

The fishing trip was *excellente* beyond words. We landed marlin, tuna, barracuda, mahi-mahi and wahoo. Carlos' friends up north were courteous and helpful, and knew the special fishing spots that only old-time fishermen would know. We supplied the cold San Miguel, and they fixed us with barbeque and kilos of fresh crab and lobster. We also spent a night in the harbor of the northern most island, Maug Island (Guam spelled backwards). On the way back, after an all-clear signal, we made a quick stop on Farallon de Mendinilla, where the US and Japanese military forces practice their aerial bombing runs.

We were about three days out when Zeke started talking about Marcella. He wanted all the details. She was a single mother with two great kids, almost teenagers now. Her husband had divorced her and moved back to Illinois. She hadn't heard from him in over five years, so he was out of the picture. She had a few boyfriends along the way but no one current. There wouldn't be jealous boyfriends hanging around with a sharp machetes or double-barreled shotguns.

Zeke had to know, "Why did her husband dump her?"

I said, "I don't know. Don't care. She's a good lady."

We were trolling. He said, "Hey, the fishing is outrageously good. We've got enough fish for us and three seafood markets. When are we heading back?"

I said, "Soon. You've got a bad case of Marcella."

Continuin' On

"I know. And it feels good." He was having trouble concentrating on baiting his hook.

Jed, Carlos and Arnie just kept smiling. We pulled in some more fish. I said, "Okay boys. We are loaded. Let's head south to Saipan."

Zeke laughed and screamed at the horizon. He was free from the past and ready to move on. The massive ocean and the never-ending horizon will put one's tiny problems in perspective plenty fast.

We had only been gone for a week, but Cocina, Marcella and the hotel crew had a grand "welcome" home party. I noticed a few more single felines in the crowd. This was going to confuse the hell out of Zeke, and probably move Jed into a decision mode.

Arnie and Guangman got the fish out of the hold. After splitting the catch and filling up our hotel's freezers, Zeke exclaimed, "I've got it. I don't wanna leave paradise and go to the smog and congestion of the mainland. I'm going to be a fisherman."

Zeke looked over at Arnie and said, "Can you help me? Can you work with me?"

Arnie said, "Zeke, that's what I do. Yep, I can work with you. I know where I can sell the leftover fish right now. All the major hotels want fresh fish for their guests."

We all showered and put on our new aloha shirts. The party was wonderful under a full moon and the Beachologist's special music and Hawaiian singers. Zeke talked to Marcella for hours and hours, and the last we saw of them, they were strolling arm-in-arm along the beach. Cocina had introduced him and Jed to several other ladies, but nothing clicked. Zeke had told Cocina that it was "love at first sight" with Marcella. He asked her how she felt. It was the same. A hot tropical romance was simmering away.

Jed had found a friend to talk to, Ms Loretta Reyes. She wouldn't be a threat to his marriage. She was a Filipina *tom-boy*, a lesbian whose lover was still in the Philippines. Cocina liked to refer to their relationship as "friendship at first sight." They were inseparable for the next two weeks, going out to dinner, going shopping and out to massage together. We expected to spot them at the beauty parlor getting pedicures and manicures.

We kidded Jed about him being the irresistible force getting her back to men for love and sex. He said that she had liked hanging out with the guys since she was a child, and had never had sex with a man. She was attracted to women just like her male friends were. He said it was so weird when she would point out a beautiful girl with a bubble butt, and say, "That would a fun one to snuggle up with." In her current relationship, she was the strong, aggressive mate, while her partner was cute and cuddly. Her girl friend had never had a man either and wasn't interested. They wanted a child and were thinking of ways to impregnate the feminine partner.

Jed said, "How about me? I'll volunteer."

"We're not going get her pregnant that way. She might decide that a *chili* feels better than a smooth vibrator."

He said, "Keep me in mind. Always ready to do community service."

Zeke and Marcella came by the penthouse with their big news. They had decided to get married, and had already contacted George and Jo for getting their license and using the wedding chapel.

I said, "Zeke, when you move, you move fast. Do you guys really know each other all that well?" Bad form, I started sounding like a father to my baby brother.

Continuin' On

He said, "We know. Everything fits. I already love her children. She has a green card, so there's no immigration problems."

I looked at Marcella and said, "How do you know that he's not a serial killer from California? How will you feel when he goes off fishing for a week at a time?"

She smiled, "I know he's a good man 'cause you and Cocina vouch for him, and he's tender and loving. Fishing is no problem. I love fishing and will go with him."

Cocina had to say, "Yeah, but you get seasick?"

Marcella said, "No problem. Just watch the horizon and feel the fresh air."

I said, "Well, let's celebrate. Hey, Annie, get out the champagne. When's the big day?"

He said, "Next Saturday. We want you and Jed to be the best men, and Cocina to be the maid of honor."

Annie asked, "What's my job? What do I do?"

"You sweet daughter need to keep the cold champagne flowing, and find some juices for you, and Anthony and Donna. In fact, go get Marcella's kids, and we'll have an impromptu party on the balcony, and watch the sun go down."

The wedding was beautiful. Everyone was dressed in Kaylene's island designs, and smelling fine in flowery leis and mwar-mwars. One of Zeke's son, James, found the time and money to fly out for the wedding, and made it to the ceremony, just as the judge said, "You may kiss the bride." He gave his dad a big hug, and welcomed Marcella to the Zeke Parker family. We got a room for James, and Jed moved in with him, allowing the newlyweds some privacy.

Jed decided to go home and work on his marriage. He was chipper and looked healthier and stronger. We said our goodbyes at the hotel, and Loretta took him to the airport. I saw tears in both their eyes. It was the essence of an unusual friendship but very intense indeed. He told her that he would be back to see the new baby. James stayed over for two weeks but had to get home to his job building roads in the High Sierra Mountains.

Zeke found a great sale on a fishing boat with an emergency outboard motor. He and Arnie went partners. Zeke had the financing and work ethic, and Arnie had the knowledge and skills. Within days, they worked out accounts at about ten hotels, with the Hyatt telling them to bring all the fish they could catch.

While we were admiring the new boat, Marcella walked over wearing her new fishing garb. She was wearing khaki military pants with a dozen pockets, a long-sleeve white T-shirt and a fishing vest which had another dozen pockets. Her bucket hat was adorned with trout flies. She had obviously been ordering out of one of those outdoors catalogs. She was serious about going fishing with the boys. Arnie and Zeke were decked out in old ratty tank tops and year-old surfer shorts.

I had to remind Zeke that the Beach Hotel got first choice on the catch. Marcella was standing by, smiling. She said, "Tom, what you and Cocina did for me and Zeke was so special. I don't think I'll ever be able to repay you…but we'll start with you always get first choice on the catch."

I laughed and said, "Good on ya." We shook hands. I told her how much I admired her new fishing clothes.

She chuckled and said, "Yeah I know. I do look pretty darn good."

All the chatter about boating and fishing brought back vivid memories of our Aussie friends, Herb and Lynda Carson, their ashes now resting in the sands of their favorite beach near

Continuin' On

Adelaide. What a wonderful memory of our times together.

As always, I looked forward to tomorrow on our beautiful island of Saipan with my family and friends. It was so good to reunite with the bros. It was especially satisfying that Zeke had decided to stay on and work out a new life with Marcella.

Time to kick back with a Filipino Corona and a smooth, golden Mexican tequila. Skip that. Might be more fun to go and find Cocina.

31

MAMA-SAN AND THE GIRLS

Mama-San Chang had been bringing her wealthy Japanese clients to two of the back rooms of our hotel for over a year, trouble free. She had rented the two rooms on a monthly basis. Sometimes the clients would slip away to Mama-San's Garapan business, while their wives were shopping, and even the single men didn't want to be seen with prostitutes. It was a very discreet operation. Our staff and guests were not allowed to hire Mama-San's ladies or visit the rooms at the hotel. Mama-San had her own cleaning and maintenance services.

Mama-San's two special girls, and the favorites of most of the clients were Wang Ren and Little Ling. They loved their work, and were thrifty businesswomen, in that they kept their living expenses at a minimum and had bank savings accounts. They never held back Mama-San's share of the service fee. As did Mama-San, they sent money home monthly for their families in China. Ernie Martines and I had visited the same two girls at Mama-San's massage parlor before we were married and

Continuin' On

had made monogamous commitments to our wives.

Often, Ren and Ling would stay over at the hotel after their clients had left. They'd pop by the restaurant and have lunch or do their calisthenics and runs on the beach. They were magnificent creatures with athletically toned bodies and beautiful faces with no skin blemishes. They spoke Mandarin Chinese, English and Japanese. They were trying to learn Korean from Guangman. Many of their lessons were cut short when Guangman's wife, Seuchill, would bounce into the restaurant after her beach run, and give the evil eye to Guangman. If that didn't slow down the lessons, then Seuchill would send daughter Bora to go sit on "Daddy's lap." He got the message and so did the ladies, and the Korean language lessons kinda faded away.

I always enjoyed "talking story" with the ladies, especially on bright days on the beach. Their eyes were squinted from the sun and when I made them laugh, their eye lids looked closed. I asked Ren, "How you see, with your eyes closed?"

She said, "I can still see out. No problem."

Ling said, "How come you not come see us? We no longer see you, Ernie and Carlos. You are good guys. Come see us at the massage parlor."

I smiled, "You know we all got married. If we come back, the wives get real mad, and cut off our dingdongs."

Ren said, "Ling's just kidding around. We all like Cocina. She is very good to us."

I said, "How's business?"

Ling said, "Still good. Economy bad. But you know what, men always have to buy food and gasoline, and if they don't get loving at home, we are necessary expense."

"That's for sure. What else is going on?"

Ren answered, "You know that Chinese girl killed last week? The one that had her throat cut and thrown out of a car in tourist area?"

I said, "Yeah. Carlos was telling me about it. What's the story?"

Ren grimaced and said, "Big mistake. The killers got wrong girl."

I said, "How do you know what happened. Was she a friend?"

Ren answered, "Yeah. I know her. She was killed instead of her roommate. Her name was Jea Chong. The killers wanted to kill Chiu Chong. The girls were sisters."

I asked, "Why did the killers want to kill anyone? Were the killers Chinese, like the girls?"

Ling said, "It happens when you don't turn in your money to Mama-San. She has to pay the local tong leader, and some money goes back to Beijing."

"How do you know all this?"

"There are no secrets in Chinese society. But people are very quiet. Chiu Chong had already been beaten up by local bosses as a warning. She almost died."

Ling said, "When she healed and went back to work, she had to work free for a month. Then when she started to get a percentage of her client fee, she wanted more, and did secret deals with regular clients without Mama-San knowing, and she kept all her tips. She supposed to give Mama some of tips."

I said, "What happened then?"

Ling continued, "The tong boss named Mr. Woo sent two assassins down to Saipan to kill her. The information they received was all wrong, and they took her sister Jea from the house. They

Continuin' On

beat and raped her in the mountains, and then cut her throat. She was thrown out in the tourist district as a message to all the other girls." She added, "It was very sad. The dead girl had been turning in her percentage to Mama-San."

"What happened to Chiu? Is she still alive?"

Ren said, "We don't know, but we heard she escaped to Guam on a boat last month."

I said, "And I suppose the killers are long gone?"

"Oh yeah, of course. The killers come in as tourists, and leave a day or two later."

"I suppose there is a lesson there to be learned. Turn in your money and avoid deals without Mama-San."

Ren said, "I learned that when I first started with another Mama-San. She got beat up for not turning in part of her share to the tong bosses. They made her work for free when the navy ships came in."

I said, "It's a tough business with its own rules."

Ren said, "It's okay when you know the rules. Everybody gets a fair share."

Ling interjected and said, "We liked your brother Jed."

"How did you get to know him?"

She said, "He gave us visits after our clients left. He liked massages with happy endings. Sometimes we would both massage him all over. He wanted us completely naked. He liked us to masturbate for him."

I said, "Here at the hotel? Did he tell you he was married?"

"He said it was okay because we wouldn't be noisy. We thought you knew. He said he was married, but blow jobs and hand jobs didn't count, because that wasn't sex or fucking."

"It's not sex?"

Ren said, "No, not sex. One of your presidents said it wasn't sex."

I said, "Yep, that happened. Did he pay you?"

Ren said, "No money, and we told Mama-San. He took us to dinner though, and bought us some nice bath gel and perfume. We really liked him. It was like a date."

Walking back to my penthouse, I thought about the unfortunate sister killed by mistake. I also felt empathy for her family back home with their loss of income. They might never learn about their daughters and their disappearances. Two missing girls out of over a billion people in China wouldn't cause much government concern.

Then I found myself grinning about the middle brother, Jed. He finally got to see another pussy. He was the quiet one, and was out enjoying life in his own way. Zeke and I thought he was doing meditation and trying to figure out his marriage situation. At least now he had some perspective on how he wanted to live out the rest of his life.

Jed had flagrantly and blatantly violated hotel rules concerning fraternization between the ladies, and hotel guests and residents. Maybe I'd give him a break this time. He probably never had a chance to read the hotel rules.

As I knew from my own past history, massages with happy endings take away all the worries of the world. Maybe Major General Joseph "Fighting Joe" Hooker of the Civil War knew something about keeping his Union troops satisfied and motivated.

32

FUNNY MONEY – STRANGE LITTLE MAN

Myla first noticed the weird looking US one hundred dollar notes when a Korean man paid his hotel bill and checked out. She thought that they felt funny, with less cotton that regular US bills, and the color wasn't exactly the same. The serial numbers were also consecutive or very close in the numbering system. She compared them to some "Ben Franklins" on hand, and with some of the other bills offered by the Korean, and they just weren't right.

The man was Shu Song, on the way to Guam for a few days with his family, and then back to Saipan to finish out his holiday. The FBI responded to the hotel and took a quick look at the bills, using their special scopes and written "what to look for" tip sheets. The agents thought they might be counterfeit bills. FBI Agent Bill Hawking called the Secret Service agents on Guam, who have jurisdiction over counterfeiting, and asked them to intercept Mr. Song when he got off the plane. It was only a forty minute flight so the agents moved quickly to make their interception.

They found Mr. Song after he cleared immigration on Guam. He didn't fit the profile of someone trying to pass fake money. He accompanied the agents to a private area, and was more than willing to show the agents all the money that he was carrying. Mrs. Song came along, and showed the agents her one hundred dollar bills, as did Mr. Song, about $2700 total. Nine of the bills looked suspicious to the agents, and they asked if they could write a receipt and take them to their main office for a thorough examination. Mr. Song agreed.

The conclusions issued by the office crime lab was definite. All nine bills were counterfeit, very well done, and just part of a massive effort from North Korea to negatively impact the world's economy and increase the profits of the North Korea political machine through its illicit activities.

One of the problems with counterfeit money is that once it is seized for investigation and evidence, the value of the money for the possessor is lost. The victim isn't reimbursed with legitimate bills. Of course, this accounts for mostly honest people trying to pass the phony bills again after they discover them in their wallets, before the bank or police can confiscate them. No one wants to be a sucker.

Mr. Song was shocked when he heard his money was being seized. He said that he had gone to a backstreet money changer in Seoul before his flight, who offered a better rate for his won (usually about 920 won to $1.00). He had also bought some name brand American cigarettes from the money changer. Agent Garcia picked them up, turned them over a few times, did a sniff, and said, "Mr. Song, he also sold you counterfeit cigarettes.

Continuin' On

These are homegrown cigarettes made in North Korea."

Secret Service Agent John Griffin explained what they knew about the North Korea crime operation. He said, "There's a conglomerate of buildings in Pyongyang called Daesong Bureau 39. It houses and directs all the North Korean criminal activities throughout the world, and is run by North Korea Dictator Kim Jong-Il. It's here where Kim and his high-placed government subordinates created a crime syndicate close to a Mafia operation, but larger and more worldwide. It involves fake goods, counterfeiting money, and growing and selling opium and making methamphetamines. Last year, about ten factories turned out forty-one billion fake name-brand cigarettes made from local tobacco. They make near-perfect one hundred bills, which they turn into hard currency, all in conjunction with Iran."

Mr. Song said, "Yes but...I exchanged the bills in South Korea from a South Korean guy."

Agent Garcia said, "Where there's money to be made, someone will always step up, and in this case, a South Korean shafted another South Korean. Criminals have no feeling of loyalty, they just want money. They just slip the phony bills over the border and start exchanging. Right now, it is estimated that North Korea has issued about forty-five million dollars in funny money out into the marketplace."

"What can I do? Nine hundred dollars is a big loss."

Agent Griffin said, "You can start by watching that crazy guy Kim up north. He's really set on developing nuclear missiles."

Mr. Song said, "He's nuts and very dangerous. He's short and fat, and wears platform shoes and has a bouffant hair-do just to make himself look taller. He's got some mental health issues. I work in the medical field, and to us, he's a big joke. But I suppose he is a very dangerous buffoon. You have to listen to anyone who might have nuclear capability. He doesn't have feelings for other people, and watched about three million North Koreans die of starvation and diseases who could have been treated. He's totally narcissistic and often rounds up women to serve in his pleasure brigades, locked "fun" rooms for himself and his aides."

"That's what we learned. He hands out favors and women, and lots of cash to keep his top echelon loyal. And if that doesn't work, he just kills off his adversaries."

He added, "He's capable of just about anything. Even though he's now sixty-five years old, he's still a spoiled brat. He's liable to give weapons of mass destruction to terrorists to use against the US and its allies. He's already exporting ballistic missiles to Iran."

Mr. Song was thanked for his cooperation and sent on his way. Fortunately he had a credit card if he ran short of vacation cash. His counterfeit cigarettes and his phony bills were held for evidence. A precise report would be sent to the South Korea authorities for follow-up, particularly dealing with money-changers around the airport. The FBI dropped by our hotel, and confiscated five one-hundred bills from Myla. As in any crooked scheme, many people are affected. I prepared advisory bulletins for all the hotels on Saipan and Guam. We have a lot of tourists from South Korea. It later developed that the CNMI Customs inspectors had already confiscated over three hundred cases of counterfeit cigarettes from 40' containers on ships registered in Panama.

I watched the news about the negotiations by the United Nations with North Korea and its nuclear capability. There was no doubting that the world knew about North Korea's criminal activity, and wanted China and South Korea to step up its inspections of ships leaving North Korea. Japan recently seized a ship

Continuin' On

with 3300 pounds of crystal meth, and Australia stopped a North Korea vessel with $45 million street value of high grade heroin.

There were no more reports of funny money to the local authorities. Maybe it was just a one-time thing for Saipan and Guam, and most of the funny money was floating around in Asia.

For survival, the world was focused in on controlling Kim's nuclear capabilities, and his distribution of all types of weapons. New Jersey authorities had just busted an organized crime syndicate from China, dealing in North Korean counterfeit money, illegal drugs, and contraband cigarettes, and most significially, over one million dollars worth of pistols, machine guns and rocket launchers. It was feared that Kim might be transferring nuclear technology to terror groups such as Al Qaeda and Hezbollah.

The funny money made it apparent that there was no escaping dangerous despots like Kim, or Bashar Al-Assad, Mahmoud Ahmadinejad, or the clown Hugo Chavez, even on sleepy little Pacific islands. If counterfeit money can get to Saipan, why not WMD and biological weapons. Security was doubled at the seaport every time that Navy destroyers and submarines came in for refitting and refueling. Closer checks were made of all the containers on planes and ships.

But who would control the jabbering of the young submarine sailor in the throes of lust with his *puta?* The pillow talk afterwards would be relayed to mama-san, who would inform her handler, and then passed on to the tong boss. Information about the technology of the ship and the movements of the crew could easily be sold or traded.

Loose lips sink ships, and maybe the entire naval base!

33

THE COMMISH

Commissioner Lois Harding was keeping the Police Department together and holding herself together, through all the political intrigue and challenges of the past year. The marijuana field murders and the assassinations had put tons of pressure on her to solve the crimes. The culprits had been arrested for the murders of the six victims that we had found buried on the marijuana plantation. With the exception of Ricardo Zambales, now in federal prison, the assassinations had no clear solution.

It was discovered through INTERPOL that the Chinese man and woman buried in the same grave had ties to one of the Chinese tongs from Beijing. However, there was no proof to substantiate this information and it was passed off as theory only. The Crime Stoppers organization increased the reward to ten thousand dollars for information leading to the identification and arrest of the assassins, but no one stepped forward, and no member of the organization had posted the rewards information in the Chinese language. Since the assassin's victims

Continuin' On

had been locals, there were dozens of calls and contacts by the local families to the governor demanding results in the investigation. The media was after answers every day.

During this turmoil, Lois was still trying to manage a 140-person police department. She wasn't given an adequate budget, and with the downturn of the economy, crime was steadily on the increase, especially armed robberies. Rather than looking at the reality of resources, fifty of the Department members circulated a petition requesting that the governor fire the commissioner for her incompetence.

Lois' husband got fed up with the whole mess and the pressure on Lois and their family, and started job hunting on the mainland. He was working as a lawyer for Micronesian Legal Services, also limping along with inadequate funding. His résumé hit the internet, and within three weeks after telephone interviews, he was offered a job in Louisville, Kentucky, at twice the pay. Lois' contract had about ten months to run out. She asked her hubby to be patient and hang in a little longer. He thought about it for three days, and then told her that he was going. He offered to take their three children with him, and she could join them later.

Lois was angry and upset, feeling that everyone was letting her down. She went over to the gym and banged the hell out of the heavy bag. She and I had developed a good relationship over morning coffee in the Beach Hotel Restaurant, talking about cases and some of her problem children on the job. She called after her gym workout, and asked, "Can we get together? I need to talk."

I said, "The Starbuck Kenya coffee will be brewing in less than ten minutes. Come on over for a chat. We provide all services at our hotel, including counseling and gossip. Ready for the good news? Guangman has been baking again – maybe some little pastries with strawberry filling."

Lois strolled into the coffee bar in about fifteen minutes. She was freshly showered and not displaying all the stress that been coming her way. We hugged.

I said, "Okay, woman. Lay it out. What's going on at the cop shop?"

She filled me in on the personal stuff, and then the professional job stuff. I said, "First you have to understand. The day that you slide out of the commissioner's chair, some other person will slide in. It may be bad choice. It may be some incompetent, political animal. But it's not your problem."

She answered, "I know all that, Tom, in my logical brain. But there's a part of me that never lets anyone down, or leaves a job unfinished. My mama taught me to work hard and be successful. I really want to help these people and make the island a better and safer place. It's corny, I know."

"Not corny. That's what makes you a good person, and a good administrator. You care about your troops and the community. But you have to know when to cut your losses, like the old cliché, "ya gotta know when to hold 'em, and when to fold 'em." Do you wanna put your family through more hassle or maybe even lose your family over a job which won't mean shit in a coupla of years? Who knows, they might fire you anyway, today or maybe tomorrow."

"That's what my honey said too. He wants me to go with him now."

"Look, it's real simple. People first came to these islands about four thousand years ago. Then Magellan and the rest of the colonizers arrived, and you know what, the people and the islands

Continuin' On

have survived. Life goes on, with or without us outsiders."

She said, "Message received loud and clear, Tom. I really tried my best." She started to tear up. This was a good woman, and a strong police leader.

"And your best was par excellence. Improvements were made and cases solved. You got rid of some real jerks on the department. You developed some good future administrators and investigators."

"Yeah, you're right. My family is the most important thing in my life. What kind of notice should I give?"

I said, "You've got the best reason, your family. You know how important "family" is to islanders. The bosses will understand, and many of them will be glad to see you in the wind and on the plane to the mainland."

I watched her leave the hotel. Her shoulders were slightly slumped but she still had the determined gait to her walk. The islands and the government bureaucracies will chew up good people like her, if they stay too long. People come from all over the world with great intentions about making progress, but sometimes islanders regard progress differently than the industrialized nations.

In Lois's case, she hadn't become an alcoholic, or developed hypertension, or lost her family. She left walking tall, and knowing that she had made a difference in making the islands a little safer.

Cocina and her crew organized a nice going-away party for just our families and close friends. Carlos had already turned in his badge and ID card, telling her that he didn't want to work with the new police bosses. Through the local coconut express, Carlos had already heard about a new appointment. Lois told everyone thanks for their help, and invited one and all to visit her family in Kentucky.

Cocina and I helped the family to get to the airport on departure day. As she left, she slipped a note in my hand. It read:

> Dear Tom,
>
> I will never forget you and Cocina and Carlos for helping me every day. And I will never forget our runs along the sandy beaches, enjoying the sapphire sea and the swaying palms, and solving the problems of the world. It was good to have a confidant and mentor.
>
> Aloha and Mahalo.
>
> Lois and Family

What we had dreaded, happened the next day. The governor appointed one of his campaign cronies to the commissioner's position. The new man had no police or fire-fighting experience, but had a lot of friends who had made sizable contributions at the last election and offered free trips to Hong Kong and Manila. Lois' hard work would go down the proverbial drain. The police officers dismissed by Lois were expecting phone calls next day to come back to work.

More of the same BS was coming up. The foreign investors would take note of the instability and corruption of the government...and keep their money at home.

I suppose that sometimes it has to get worse before it gets better. Politicians prosper when good people remain quiet. And these politicians do not want competition from truth and honesty.

I told Cocina, "I might run for office and gets things squared away."

She laughed and said, "And how big is your island family? How many voters do you have, Big Boy?"

"I've got you, Babe."

34

THE LAST ASSHOLE

Zambales made his plea bargain and was off to the supermax Federal Prison in Colorado for violent offenders, and for inmates under protective custody. He had already been labeled a snitch through the prison grapevine, so his chances of surviving his twenty-five years sentence were unlikely. For his own protection, Zambales was facing long years of solitary confinement.

Zambales was a violent, nasty person. There was no excuse for his criminal behavior, but there was an explanation or some understanding in how he had evolved as a sociopathic human being. The victims and their families wouldn't understand or give a shit about his childhood. He was an evil person and probably should have been executed and taken off the face of the planet. The only reason that he decided to help the prosecution was to save his own worthless hide. He adjusted to his circumstances, and would probably find religion in the prison. By going to church, he could get fresh baked cookies and two evenings of fresh air.

As a struggling child, Zambales had been beaten constantly by both his mother and father for the most minor violation of family rules. His mother and father were often away from home living their dishonest and illegal lives, while Zambales often went without food, but was afraid of another beating if he left the house to go beg for food. Vitamins and nourishment were foreign words in his house.

His mother often brought home her lovers, and if the father was away selling drugs on nearby islands and Guam, his mother and the most recent lover would fornicate and drink all night. Sometimes the men beat his mother because they were all screwed-up and drunk, or the mother was not performing to their standards. The next day, the mother would take out his anger on the boy.

By this time, he was damaged goods, a social cripple. He had no concept of right or wrong, just survival.

When the boy reached puberty, his mother caught him masturbating. She saw that he was well-endowed. From that point on, his mother would tell her girl friends that her boy had a giant prick. She'd call the boy into the kitchen, and tell him to drop his pants, so the ladies could see his penis. She even tried to give him a handjob, so the ladies could see him pumped up. He ran away in embarrassment, while the ladies were cackling about the size of his penis.

Zambales got in the habit of peeping at his female neighbors while they were showering. He stole panties and brassieres from their clothes lines. He was caught masturbating by one of the husbands while he looking through a window at nighttime, and was nearly beaten to death. The police came and hauled him away. He didn't receive medical attention until the next day. Future

Continuin' On

medical evaluators said that the beating and the lack of prompt medical treatment had probably caused neurological damage. Even the most menial of activities made him a nervous wreck. He was immature and irresponsible. A Chinese philosopher would say, "He has met his destiny. There is no turning back."

People of his ilk seem to find other misfits. There are formal psychological and sociological terms for his condition. A veteran cop would simply describe him "all fucked up," which he was.

Zambales fell in with Juan Rivera's crowd, and was soon using and selling marijuana. He graduated to amphetamines, and discovered that he could trade drugs for sex. He liked to go to the public markets or to concerts, and brag to his cohorts that he had "fucked that one" and point out other girls and say, "Yeah, I fucked her too. And I fucked her sister." He would see a pregnant girl, and say, "I knocked her up. She's carrying my kid."

Zambales lived in a fantasy world, and most of his cohorts knew that he was a braggart. If it wasn't for the drugs, Zambales would never have gotten laid. The other gang members looked down on him, and used him for gofer jobs, or drug contacts that were dangerous. He always seemed to survive until he got caught up with the gang rape of Mei on the beach, and followed Rivera's lead in the rape and murders of the six victims in the marijuana field. He was spiraling down and there was no coming back. It was a just a matter of time, just as Woo had told Chow and Ling.

His snitching gave him a lifetime reputation. Every con in the Colorado prison knew who he was. He was spotted outside his cell several times in the medical office or at the church by the other inmates. He usually had a corrections officer with him. No one would talk to him, except for the prison staff who had no choice. Snitches never look down the line after their tattle-taling, never realizing no one respects snitches, not even the investigators who used them for their information.

Several months went by. Prison life became routine, and Zambales found religion and decided he should enroll in a GED program. His food came every day to his cell, transported from a food cart by trusted long-term cons. On the second anniversary of the Woo's god-daughter's murder, Zambales anxiously awaited his dinner. It was beef stroganoff night, and he was looking forward to a good meal. It also meant that there would be apple pie and coffee for dessert.

Zambales dove into his meal. He thought the pie and coffee were little off in taste. Two hours later, he was sweating and thrashing on his bunk. He was yelling for help but no one came. His plate and coffee cup had already been picked up, and washed within minutes. The video surveillance camera recorder had been disabled and broken for a week. The officers in the control booth were busily playing pinochle and weren't watching the video screens. Zambales began to convulse and cramp, and liquid feces flowed out his anus. He vomited yellow puss and blood, and his dying thoughts were of Chinese demons tearing apart his body. He slipped off into oblivion and knew there was no coming back.

On a routine cell check on the hour, the officers found Zambales dead. Medical personnel responded but it was way too late. The staff had read the reports on Zambales and accepted his death as just another butthole gone to hell. His cell was scrubbed clean and another inmate was in the private cell within the day.

The prison investigators found no witnesses of any kind about anything. The autopsy later showed huge doses of arsenic in Zambales' system, especially in his hair follicles. Arsenic is

Continuin' On

basically odorless and tasteless and many people in history have been poisoned during their afternoon tea or coffee. One of the armchair prison administrators naively asked how arsenic could get into the prison. The investigators just shrugged, but knew if the cons could get in heroin and speed, why not arsenic or other poisons.

Zambales had no listed next-of-kin. No one claimed his body. He was buried the following week in the pauper section of the prison graveyard. They sent off his few personal possessions to the Salvation Army.

On the day of the poisoning, Tong Boss Woo received a brief, timely notification. He told the messenger that his loan was forgiven, and would enjoy seeing him on their next trip to Shanghai. He was enjoying a fresh pot of green tea from his newest plantations.

Woo settled back in his chair. He had very, very large sums of money, and thousands of square kilometers of land. At times like this, revenge was sweeter than money and possessions, and the finest wine. Eight down – none to go. His god-daughter could now rest at peace in the heavens.

He summoned his eunuch, and told him to bring the two little country girls. He wanted them wearing the sparkly face tattoos, and nothing else. It was truly an exhilarating day.

EPILOGUE

Saipan had broken out in peace and harmony. For the past month, nothing spectacular happened and that's the way we like it. I was enjoying my endless summer. One day just blended into the next. I mastered various degrees of sail-boarding and body surfing. Sometimes I got tangled in the ropes. Cocina admonished me about my swearing around the children. My argument that cops just talk that way wasn't working. I knew it was getting bad, when Cocina overheard one of the neighbor children, four-year-old Alice Ping shout, "Oh shit!" when she saw me do a header into a six-foot wave.

With the former commissioner gone to the mainland, the majority of felonies were put away in some dark file, including the unsolved assassinations. Many of the crime victims were tourists from Japan or China, and wouldn't be around to make a complaint about little or no investigation, and even if the case was solved, very few victims would ever return and rehash the whole crime while testifying in court.

Continuin' On

Daisy had kept me informed as to the events in the Chinese community, but usually in the aftermath. There was never any advance warning. From second and third accounts from people that heard everything through distant cousins, she explained precisely how and where the assassins had worked and what their missions were. She said that we needn't worry because their work was done, unless certain situations had to be addressed, such as disciplining an employee in the vice underworld, or a horrific violation against a Chinese in the community. There was no intention in taking over all the crime in the CNMI through triads and tongs. The islands were very small, and there wasn't much money to be made.

Carlos and I only had a few minor cases. We used some of the spare time to go fishing and photograph the volcanoes up north on the remote islands. The rest of the time, we did some cross-country motorcycle riding, and took up tennis with Jonah. Guangman continued his fine meals, and I found myself trying on my old police uniform more often, just to make sure it still fit. When the middle button started to bulge, it was time for "push-aways" from the table, and more running time on the sand. If Cocina got involved in the tummy issue, I knew dinner was going to be carrots, cucumbers and plenty of tomatoes.

After dinner, I enjoyed sitting on the balcony, and watching the sun set the sky on fire. Saipan is a special place to be on the planet. It's like the planets and stars were all aligned in exact symmetry, and Mother Nature gave us a view of heaven before our time. I know that we pass the anniversary date of our own death unawares every year. When my time came, I wanted to make sure that my life had been full of expeditions and adventure, and love. I liked the simple life of friendships and family, and a fresh cup of Guatemala coffee, and laughing and giggling with the children. But I still wanted to climb Mount Fuji and raft the spring rivers of New Zealand.

Cocina came out on the porch and said, "Well Big Fella, looks like you're enjoying your beach and the fire sky."

"Yeah. What did I do in this life, or former life, to have all of this? The beauty and serenity and you, mi corazon."

"Now Slick-Talker, what going on in your little pea-brain? Are you hoping to get lucky?" Wow, I loved this woman and all her slang. She'd be an American even before her naturalization papers came through.

I said, "I already got lucky. You married me, poor foolish little girl."

"Glad I did." She smiled and pursed her lips in a kiss. She went inside the house to help the kiddies with their homework. I heard Hawaiian slack-key guitar music from inside. That meant only one thing—it was Donna's turn to clear the table and do the dishes, and she was singing and dancing as she went about her chores.

I looked down at the beach. Lola was stacking the beach chairs. Yoshi was tending to his plants. The sand was now red like the sky and the Philippine Sea. I was still battling the thoughts that something was bound to go wrong. It was all too perfect. This piece of paradise and personal happiness could not endure.

I listened to the gently swaying palms and recalled something important from my friends, the paniolos on Hawaii. I remembered their exact words. Cowboys are great philosophers around a campfire. "Today is over, and tomorrow, let's wait and see what happens, and we'll handle whatever comes along." Meanwhile, sip your Manila brandy.

Continuin' On

Happy anniversary grim reaper, but not until next year. That's good rationale. I agree. No fucking cancer allowed.
Okay then Bucko. Relax and be happy. See ya at the next round-up.

GLOSSARY

(SPANISH—ESPANOL UNLESS OTHERWISE NOTED)

Americano	American—sometimes Kano (Filipino)
Amigo	friend, compadre
Animales	animals, less than human
Arigatoo	thank you (Japanese)
Arriba	up, onward
Atulai, tataga, & mafute	reef fish (Chamorro)
Ay naku	Oh no!—kind of like Spanish Caramba! (Filipino)
Azul	blue
Bakla	male homosexual (Filipino)
Banzai	cheers, best wishes (Japanese)

Continuin' On

Barong Tagalog	Filipino white shirt worn outside the trousers
Basug	full with food (Filipino)
Bebe	vagina (Chamorro – Hawaiian)
Ben Franklin	$100 American bill
Biba Marianas	hooray for the Marianas Islands
Bruja	witch, evil spirit
Ca-ca	feces, excrement, shit – sometimes spelled ka-ka (European derivative)
Calabozo	jail, carcel
Cannabis sativa	marijuana, weed, ganja, Mary Jane, grass
Caramba!	Good lord, damn it
Casa	home
Cebuan	a lady from Cebu, Philippines
Chamorita	young Chamorro girl
Chica	young girl
Chili	penis (Chamorro)
Ciudad	city
CNMI	Commonwealth of the Northern Marianas Islands
Cojones	balls, testicles
Corazon	heart, sweetheart
Crispy Pata Baboy	baked pig's knuckles made crispy

Cristo	Jesus Christ
Daijo obu tassuke-te	Wait, we're going for help (Japanese)
Domo	thank you, showing gratitude (Japanese)
Dulce	sweet, candy
Excellente	excellent, very good
Fair dinkum	for real, authentic, benign, not cussing (Australian)
Ganja	marijuana slang from India
GPS	global positioning system (worldwide usage)
Grande	huge, large
Halfa-halfa	slang term for one-half of one race, and another half of another
Halo-halo	favorite dessert drink in the Philippines — crushed ice and fruit
Hombre	man
Ichiban	number one, the best (Japanese)
Jefe	chief
JoJo Island	center of Abu Sayyaf, Muslim terrorist group — Philippines
Kahuna	big chief (Hawaiian)
Kamote	sweet potato (Chamorro)
Kriminal	criminal, crook, bad guy
Kris	a Filipino curved knife

Continuin' On

Ladrone	thief
Lagniappe	"lan-yap" – French-Spanish-Cajun – giving something extra
Lango	drunk, intoxicated (Filipino)
Lumpia	egg rolls with meat and vegetables (Filipino)
Mabuhay	welcome, like an aloha greeting (Filipino)
Maganda	pretty, beautiful (Filipino)
Malacanang Palace	home of Filipino President
Man'amko	senior citizen (Chamorro)
Mangkukulam	witch, sometimes bad, sometimes good (Filipino)
Masarap	delicious, very tasty (Filipino)
Maven	expert, connoisseur (Yiddish)
Mindanao	southern province of Philippines
Muchacho	young lad
Muchas gracias	thank you
Munquita	cute, little doll
Nom de guerre	alias, pseudonym (French)
Nuestra Senora de La Conception	Spanish galleon, Our Lady of Conception
Origami	art of paper folding (Japanese)
P.I.	Philippine Islands – Republic of the Philippines (or private investigator)

Paniolo	cowboy (Hawaiian)
Pendejo	bad guy, asshole, jerk
Persona non grata	unacceptable person (Latin)
Pinoy	a male Filipino – female is Pinay
Posadero	hotel/inn keeper
Puki	vagina (Filipino)
Puta	prostitute, whore, prostie
Que onda?	What's up?
Que paso?	What's happening?
Quien sabe?	Who knows?
Regeno	fake weed, counterfeit
Sake	rice wine (Japanese)
Salamat po	thank you (Filipino)
Sereno	night watchman
Shabu	ice, amphetamines (Japanese)
Shao bao	meat filled dimpling (Chinese)
Si yu'us ma'ase	thank you (Chamorro)
Siempre	always
Suso	female breast (Filipino – Chamorro)
Tagalog	one of the official languages of the Philippines
Tano Antigo	ancient land, referring to CNMI (Chamorro)

Continuin' On

Terno	traditional formal Filipina dress—made famous by Imelda Marcos
Te-te	female breast (Micronesian)
Tom-boy	lesbian, lezzie (Filipino)
Tsinelas	slippers, flip-flops, zories (Filipino)
Tsismis	gossip (Filipino)
Une bonne blaque, bein?	good joke, eh? (French)
Vamonos	let's go
Vaqueros	cowboy
Yen	Japanese currency
Voir dire	examination of witness or potential jury member (Latin)
Yakuza	Japanese organized crime
Yo	delicious, tasty (Ponapeian)

ACKNOWLEDGMENTS

Writing a novel is a lonely business. Some days your protagonists want to hide out and not be bothered, like when your computer goes into hibernation. You just want to run away, and just wander and do anything, like washing the car, painting the bedroom, rechecking your income taxes, or any chore that will allow you to escape the mental anguish of staring at the blank computer screen. But then your Support Team boosts you back on track, and they jumpstart your creative juices with a cup of Japanese tea, American grilled cheese sandwiches and burgers, some cookies from the Philippines, a Bali neck massage, and emails of re-assurance.

I have to mention specifically my good friends, The Support Team, that lent a hand, with the encouragement and editing, like Joe Weaver, Juanita Mendoza, Urbano Duenas, Jeff Williams, Nancy Nielsen, Ruth Tighe, Jill Dickerson, Bud and Donna White, Johnny Bowe, Mary Miradora, Danny "Banjo-Man" Hocking, Jane Mack, John Del Nero, and others who

Continuin' On

kept the inspiration bubbling forth.

It could not have happened without the support of my *maganda* wife, Salve', and our three wonderful children, Gresil, Paila and George, and our niece, Katrina (the honor student, school politician, and grilled cheese specialist).

My friends and family have taught me to embrace a passion, and to sing and dance, and to appreciate those bursts of happiness, those special moments of joy when you know, for sure, that life is really worth living.

Thanx to one and all. I appreciate you folks big-time. Mahalo, muchas gracias, arigatoo, menlau, si yu'us ma'ase, and salamat po.

ISBN 1425143202

9 781425 143206